THOMAS THE TANK ENGINE

STORY COLLECTION

THE ISLAND OF SODOR

❋ Reference ❋

Rivers	Railway N.W.R.
Main Roads	Railway Narrow Gauge
Secondary Roads	Built-up Areas
Tracks & Boundaries	

1. Here the engines live in their shed.
2. Edward's station. He shunts here.
3. Gordon stuck on this hill.
4. Henry was shut up in this tunnel.
5. Thomas used to arrange coaches here.
6. The trucks pushed James down this hill.
7. James had his accident here.
8. This is Thomas' Junction.
9. Here James had hiccoughs!
10. James made the troublesome trucks come here.
11. Thomas left his Guard behind here.
12. Here Thomas went fishing.
13. Here Thomas stuck in the snow.
14. Thomas raced Bertie the 'bus along this valley.
15. Henry met an elephant in this tunnel.
16. James spun round on the turntable here.
17. Percy ran away from this station.
18. The 'Flying Kipper' had an accident here.
19. The quarry line, where Thomas met the policeman.
20. James bumped the tar-wagons here.
21. Mrs Kyndley's cottage.
22. Here Gordon fell in a ditch.
23. Here James slipped on the leaves.
24. Here Thomas fell down a mine.
25. Here the engines met H.M. The Queen.
26. Here Henry and Gordon met a cow.
27. Bertie the 'bus chased Edward from here.
28. Here is Trevor the Traction-engine's scrapyard.
29. James ran away from here, and Edward chased him.
30. Duck took charge of the Yard here.
31. Harold Helicopter lives at this airfield.
32. Percy brought the children through floods here.
33. Here Percy fell into the sea.
34. From here, Gordon went to London.
35. Toby ran out of water near here.
36. Here the Fat Controller spoke to the Engines before taking them to England.
37. Here Edward talked to Skarloey.
38. Here Sir Handel slipped through the rails.
39. Here is the Skarloey Railway.
40. On this viaduct, Gordon lost his dome.
41. Here Duck ran into the barber's shop.
42. Thomas' Branch-line runs from KNAPFORD to FFARQUHAR.
43. Edward's Branch-line runs from WELLSWORTH to BRENDAM.
44. Engines are made and repaired at CROVAN'S GATE.

ISLE OF MAN

RAMSEY

DOUGLAS

ARLSBURGH

CASTLETOWN

TIDMOUTH

ELSBRIDGE

KNAP-FORD

WELLS

CRUSBY

IRISH SEA

THOMAS THE TANK ENGINE

STORY COLLECTION

THE REVEREND W. AWDRY

RANDOM HOUSE
NEW YORK

The Three Railway Engines first published in Great Britain 1945

Thomas the Tank Engine first published in Great Britain 1946

James the Red Engine first published in Great Britain 1948

Tank Engine Thomas Again first published in Great Britain 1949

Troublesome Engines first published in Great Britain 1950

Henry the Green Engine first published in Great Britain 1951

Toby the Tram Engine first published in Great Britain 1952

Gordon the Big Engine first published in Great Britain 1953

Edward the Blue Engine first published in Great Britain 1954

Four Little Engines first published in Great Britain 1955

Percy the Small Engine first published in Great Britain 1956

The Eight Famous Engines first published in Great Britain 1957

Duck and the Diesel Engine first published in Great Britain 1958

The Twin Engines first published in Great Britain 1960

Thomas the Tank Engine & Friends®

A BRITT ALLCROFT COMPANY PRODUCTION

Based on The Railway Series by the Reverend W Awdry
© 2005 Gullane (Thomas) LLC
Thomas the Tank Engine and Friends and Thomas & Friends are trademarks of Gullane Entertainment Inc.
Thomas the Tank Engine & Friends is Reg. U.S. Pat. TM Off.
A HIT Entertainment Company

Library of Congress Cataloging-in-Publication Data
Awdry, W. Thomas the tank engine story collection / W. Awdry ; [C. Reginald Dalby, John T. Kenney, illustrators].
p. cm. "Based on The Railway Series by The Reverend W. Awdry."
SUMMARY: A collection of fourteen previously published stories featuring Thomas, Sir Topham Hatt, and their railway friends.
ISBN 0-375-83409-5 [1. Railroads–Trains–Fiction. 2. England–Fiction.]
I. Dalby, C. Reginald, ill. II. Kenney, John T., ill. III. Awdry, W. Railway series. IV. Title.
PZ7.A9613Thdw 2005 [E]–dc22 2005046450

First published in Great Britain 2002 by Egmont Books Limited
239 Kensington High Street, London W8 6SA

Acknowledgment: *The Gloucester Citizen* (photograph, page 8)

Book design by Clair Stutton and Janene Spencer

MANUFACTURED IN SPAIN 5 7 9 10 8 6

ISBN 0-375-83409-5

www.randomhouse.com/kids/thomas   www.thomasandfriends.com

Contents

About the Author

WILBERT VERE AWDRY was born on June 15, 1911, the son of the Reverend Vere Awdry, vicar of Ampfield, near Romsey in Hampshire. From the first, young Wilbert had a passion for steam engines. He loved to meet and chat with local railway men, to play with the model railway his father had built in the garden, and to pore over his father's copies of *The Railway Magazine*.

When Wilbert's brother, George, was born, the Awdrys moved to Box in Wiltshire, near the Great Western Railway's main line from Paddington to Bristol.

Lying in bed as a child I would hear a heavy goods train coming in and stopping at Box station, then the three whistles, crowing for a banker, a tank-engine, which would come out of his little shed to help the goods train up the gradient. There was no doubt in my mind that steam engines all had definite personalities. I would hear them snorting up the grade and little imagination was needed to hear in the puffings and pantings of the two engines the conversation they were having with one another: "I can't do it! I can't do it! I can't do it!" "Yes, you can! Yes, you can! Yes, you can!"

Wilbert went to Dauntsey School in Wiltshire and then to Oxford. When he left Oxford, he taught at St. George's school in Jerusalem, where he met his future wife, Margaret Emily Wale. Returning to England in 1936, he was ordained deacon at Winchester Cathedral and became a curate at Odiham in Hampshire. Two years later, he married Margaret, and in 1940, their first child, Christopher, was born, followed by two daughters, Veronica, in 1943, and Hilary, in 1946. When Christopher was two, he was confined to bed with measles. Wilbert entertained him with a story about a little engine who was sad. His name was Edward.

Christopher loved to hear the story of Edward again and again—and eventually his father wrote it down and illustrated it with simple line drawings. Stories about Gordon and Henry followed, and Margaret encouraged Wilbert to send the books to a publisher.

The Three Railway Engines was published by Edmund Ward in 1945, and the following year, the most famous of all Wilbert Awdry's engine characters appeared in *Thomas the Tank Engine*. From *James the Red Engine,* in 1948, Awdry published a new Railway Series title every year until his last book, *Tramway Engines*, in 1972. From the publication and success of the very first book, it was obvious that Wilbert had created a wonderful new world for children to explore. This world—in its fictional setting of the Island of Sodor, situated between the British mainland and the Isle of Man—Wilbert created with his brother George. Together they devised its people, engines, history, and geography.

As well as being a full-time clergyman and dreaming up and writing his Railway Series, Wilbert Awdry also campaigned for the preservation of various steam railways, built model railway layouts, and took railway excursions at home and abroad.

In 1965, he retired and moved with his wife to Stroud in Gloucestershire. In recognition of his services to children's literature, Wilbert was awarded an OBE in the 1996 New Year's Honors List.

Wilbert died peacefully at home in 1997, age 85.

Although he wrote his last book in the series in 1972, Awdry's creation lives on! In 1983, his son, Christopher, published *Really Useful Engines,* the first in his own series about Thomas the Tank Engine and his friends.

About the Illustrators

C. REGINALD DALBY

Self-portraits: Dalby is the man with the case, his daughter has the dog!

Dalby's fresh, funny, child-centered steam engine illustrations for the Railway Series, with their bold lines, lively energy, and bright colors, were an immediate success.

C. Reginald Dalby (the "C" was for Clarence, a name he disliked and never used) was born in Leicester in 1904. At the age of thirteen, he won a scholarship to Leicester College of Art, after which he worked for five years as a commercial designer, producing a variety of packaging designs. He painted the very first Glacier Mints Polar Bear—on the side of a delivery van! At the outbreak of the Second World War, Reginald joined the RAF and served as an intelligence officer, but after the war he was soon back in Leicester, working once again as a freelance artist.

Publisher Edmund Ward knew Dalby's work, and when an illustrator was needed for the third book in the Railway Series, *James the Red Engine*, he was a natural choice. He went on to re-illustrate the first two books—*The Three Railway Engines* and *Thomas the Tank Engine*.

There was some lively discussion between Dalby and Awdry about the illustrations—Awdry was very keen that all details on the engines be technically correct; Dalby was more concerned with creating appealing characters and compositions. This difference created illustrations with a perfect balance of technical detail and humor, color, and personality. Their collaboration ended in 1956, when Dalby illustrated his last Railway Series book, *Percy the Small Engine*.

Dalby didn't just illustrate Thomas, he continued with his commercial work as well as doing his own drawings and paintings. In 1955, he wrote and illustrated a children's book of his own, featuring Tubby the Tugboat—*Tales of Flitterwick Harbour*. He loved to travel, and to paint foreign landscapes, too—particularly Greece, Spain, and France. He died in 1983, at the age of 79, after a short illness.

John T. Kenney

Percy the Small Engine was C. Reginald Dalby's last artistic collaboration on the Railway Series. John T. Kenney, another Leicestershire man, was chosen to be his successor. Kenney's illustrations are fresh and light, with larger engines and more realistic people. And they have something more, which really pleased the author: precise draftsmanship and attention to technical detail. Awdry was delighted with Kenney's appointment as illustrator.

John Theodore Eardley Kenney was born in 1911, and, like Dalby, he trained at Leicester College of Art before working as a commercial artist. While serving in the Second World War, he made dozens of on-the-spot drawings recording the D-Day landings and the triumphant sweep across Europe which followed. After the war, Kenney returned to Leicester and met his future wife, Peggy.

He illustrated several children's books for Edmund Ward (including two children's stories of his own) before illustrating six of Awdry's Railway Series books. He created a handful of new engine characters for the series, including Donald and Douglas (the Scottish Twins) and the dastardly Diesel!

In 1962, Kenney's eyesight began to fail him, and he illustrated his last title for the series, *Gallant Old Engine*. Fortunately, he was still able to continue his work as an artist, drawing and painting—especially horses, which he loved. John Kenney died in 1972, at the age of 61. In the same year, an exhibition of his paintings was mounted in Chicago.

The Three Railway Engines

 Edward's Day Out

 Edward and Gordon

 The Sad Story of Henry

 Edward, Gordon, and Henry

The Three Railway Engines

THE REV. W. AWDRY

with illustrations by

C. REGINALD DALBY

Edward's Day Out

Once upon a time, there was a little engine called Edward. He lived in a Shed with five other engines. They were all bigger than Edward and boasted about it. "The Driver won't choose you again," they said. "He wants big, strong engines like us."

Edward had not been out for a
long time; he began to feel sad.
Just then the Driver and
Fireman came along to
start work.

The Driver looked at Edward.

"Why are you sad?" he asked.
"Would you like to come out today?"

"Yes, please," said Edward. So the Fireman lit the
fire and made a nice lot of steam.

Then the Driver pulled the lever, and Edward
puffed away.

"Peep, peep," he whistled. "Look at me now."

The others were very cross at being left behind.

16

Away went Edward to get some coaches.

"Be careful, Edward," said the coaches, "don't bump and bang us like the other engines do."

So Edward came up to the coaches very, very gently, and the shunter fastened the coupling.

"Thank you, Edward," said the coaches. "That was kind; we are glad you are taking us today."

Then they went to the station, where the people were waiting.

"Peep, peep," whistled Edward—"get in quickly, please."

So the people got in quickly, and Edward waited happily for the Guard to blow his whistle and wave his green flag.

He waited and waited—there was no whistle, no green flag. "*Peep, peep, peep, peep*—where is that Guard?" Edward was getting anxious.

The Driver and Fireman asked the Station Master, "Have you seen the Guard?" "No," he said. They

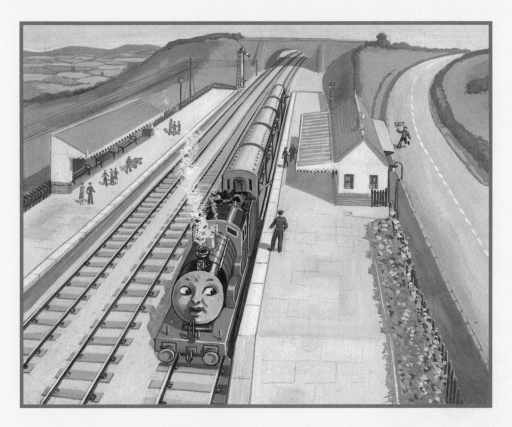

asked the porter, "Have you seen the Guard?"

"Yes—last night," said the porter.

Edward began to get cross. "Are we ever going to start?" he said.

Just then a little boy shouted, "Here he comes!" And there the Guard was, running down the hill with his flags in one hand and a sandwich in the other.

He ran onto the
platform, blew his
whistle, and jumped
into his van.

Edward puffed
off. He did have a
happy day. All the
children ran to wave as
he went past, and he met
old friends at all the

stations. He worked so hard that the
Driver promised to take him out again
the next day.

"I'm going out again tomorrow,"
he told the other engines that
night in the Shed. "What do you
think of that?"

But he didn't hear what they thought, for he was so
tired and happy that he fell asleep at once.

Edward and Gordon

One of the engines in Edward's Shed was called Gordon. He was very big and very proud.

"You watch me this afternoon, little Edward," he boasted, "as I rush through with the Express; that will be a splendid sight for you."

Just then his Driver pulled the lever. "Goodbye, little Edward," said Gordon as he puffed away, "look out for me this afternoon!"

Edward went off, too, to do some shunting.

Edward liked shunting. It was fun playing with freight cars. He would come up quietly and give them a pull.

"Oh! Oh! Oh! Oh! Oh!" screamed the freight cars. "Whatever is happening?"

Then he would stop and the silly freight cars would go bump into each other. "Oh! Oh! Oh! Oh!" they cried again.

Edward pushed them until they were running nicely, and when they weren't expecting it, he would stop; one of them would be sure to run onto another line. Edward played till there were no more freight cars; then he stopped to rest.

Presently he heard a whistle. Gordon came puffing along, very slowly, and very crossly. Instead of nice shining coaches, he was pulling a lot of very dirty coal cars.

"A goods train! A goods train! A goods train!" he grumbled. "The shame of it, the shame of it, the shame of it."

He went slowly through, with the coal cars clattering and banging behind him.

Edward laughed and went to find some more freight cars.

Soon afterwards a porter came and spoke to his Driver. "Gordon can't get up the hill. Will you take Edward and push him, please?"

They found Gordon halfway up the hill and very cross. His Driver and Fireman were talking to him severely. "You are not trying!" they told him. "I can't do it," said Gordon. "The noisy freight cars hold an engine back so. If they were coaches—clean sensible things that come quietly—now that would be different."

Edward's Driver came up. "We've come to push," he said. "No use at all," said Gordon. "You wait and see," said Edward's Driver.

They brought the train back to the bottom of the hill. Edward came up behind the brake van ready to push.

"*Peep, peep,* I'm ready," said Edward.

"*Poop, poop,* no good," grumbled Gordon.

The Guard blew his whistle, and they pulled and pushed as hard as they could.

"I can't do it, I can't do it, I can't do it," puffed Gordon.

"I will do it, I will do it, I will do it," puffed Edward.

"I can't do it, I will do it, I can't do it, I will do it, I can't do it, I will do it," they puffed together.

Edward pushed and puffed and puffed and pushed as hard as ever he could, and almost before he realized it, Gordon found himself at the top of the hill.

"I've done it! I've done it! I've done it!" he said proudly, and forgot all about Edward pushing behind. He didn't wait to say "Thank you," but ran on so fast that he passed two stations before his Driver could make him stop.

Edward had pushed so hard that when he got to the top, he was out of breath.

Gordon ran on so fast that Edward was left behind.

The Guard waved and waved, but Edward couldn't catch up.

He ran on to the next station, and there the Driver and Fireman said they were very pleased with him. The Fireman gave him a nice long drink of water, and the Driver said, "I'll get out my paint tomorrow and give you a beautiful new coat of blue with red stripes, then you'll be the smartest engine in the Shed."

The Sad Story of Henry

Once, an engine attached to a train
Was afraid of a few drops of rain—
It went into a tunnel,
And squeaked through its funnel
And never came out again.

The engine's name was Henry. His Driver and Fireman argued with him, but he would not move. "The rain will spoil my lovely green paint and red stripes," he said.

The Guard blew his whistle till he had no more breath, and waved his flags till his arms ached; but Henry still stayed in the tunnel and blew steam at him.

"I am *not* going to spoil my lovely green paint and red stripes for you," he said rudely.

The passengers came and argued, too, but Henry would not move.

Sir Topham Hatt, a director who was on the train, told the Guard to get a rope. "We will pull you out," he said. But Henry only blew steam at him and made him wet.

They hooked the rope on and all pulled—except Sir Topham Hatt. "My doctor has forbidden me to pull," he said.

They pulled and pulled and pulled, but still Henry stayed in the tunnel.

Then they tried pushing from the other end. Sir Topham Hatt said, "One, two, three, push"—but he did not help. "My doctor has forbidden me to push," he said.

They pushed and pushed and pushed, but still
Henry stayed in the tunnel.

At last another train came. The Guard waved his red
flag and stopped it. The two engine Drivers, the two
Firemen, and the two Guards went and argued with
Henry. "Look, it has stopped raining," they said. "Yes,
but it will begin again soon," said Henry. "And what
would become of my green paint with red stripes
then?"

So they brought the other engine up, and it pushed and puffed and puffed and pushed as hard as ever it could. But still Henry stayed in the tunnel.

So they gave it up. They told Henry, "We shall leave you there for always and always and always."

They took up the old rails, built a wall in front of him, and cut a new tunnel.

Now Henry can't get out, and he watches the trains rushing through the new tunnel. He is very sad

because no one will ever see his lovely green paint
with red stripes again.

But I think he deserved it, don't you?

Edward, Gordon, and Henry

Edward and Gordon often went through the tunnel where Henry was shut up.

Edward would say, "*Peep, peep*—hullo!" and Gordon would say, "*Poop, poop, poop! Serves you right!*"

Poor Henry had no steam to answer; his fire had gone out. Soot and dirt from the tunnel roof had spoiled his lovely green paint and red stripes. He was cold and unhappy, and wanted to come out and pull trains, too.

Gordon always pulled the Express. He was proud of being the only engine strong enough to do it.

There were many heavy coaches, full of important people like Sir Topham Hatt, who had punished Henry.

Gordon was seeing how fast he could go. "Hurry! Hurry! Hurry!" he panted.

"Trickety-trock, trickety-trock, trickety-trock," said the coaches.

Gordon could see Henry's tunnel in front.

"In a minute," he thought, "I'll *poop, poop, poop* at Henry and rush through and out into the open again."

Closer and closer he came—he was almost there when crack: *"Wheee——————eeshshsh."* He was in a cloud of steam and going slower and slower.

His Driver stopped the train.

"What has happened to me?" asked Gordon. "I feel so weak." "You've burst your safety valve," said the Driver. "You can't pull the train anymore."

"Oh, dear," said Gordon. "We were going so nicely, too. . . . Look at Henry laughing at me." Gordon made a face at Henry and blew smoke at him.

Everybody got out and came to see Gordon. "Humph!" said Sir Topham Hatt. "I never liked these big engines—always going wrong; send for another engine at once."

While the Guard went to find one, they uncoupled Gordon and ran him on a siding out of the way.

The only engine left in the Shed was Edward.

"I'll come and try," he said.

Gordon saw him coming. "That's no use," he said. "Edward can't pull the train."

Edward puffed and pulled and pulled and puffed, but he couldn't move the heavy coaches.

"I told you so," said Gordon rudely. "Why not let Henry try?"

"Yes," said Sir Topham Hatt, "I will."

"Will you help pull this train, Henry?" he asked. "Yes," said Henry at once.

So Gordon's Driver and Fireman lit his fire; some platelayers broke down the wall and put back the rails; and when he had steam up, Henry puffed out.

He was dirty, his boiler was black, and he was covered with cobwebs. "Ooh! I'm so stiff! Ooh! I'm so stiff!" he groaned.

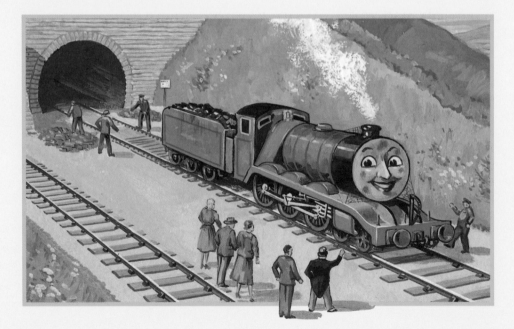

"You'd better have a run to ease your joints, and find a turntable," said Sir Topham Hatt kindly.

Henry came back feeling better, and they put him in front.

"Peep, peep," said Edward, "I'm ready."

"Peep, peep, peep," said Henry, "so am I."

"Pull hard, pull hard, pull hard," puffed Edward.

"We'll do it, we'll do it, we'll do it," puffed Henry.

"Pull hard, we'll do it, pull hard, we'll do it, pull hard, we'll do it," they puffed together. The heavy coaches jerked and began to move, slowly at first, then faster and faster.

"We've done it together! We've done it together! We've done it together!" said Edward and Henry.

"You've done it, hurray! You've done it, hurray! You've done it, hurray!" sang the coaches.

All the passengers were excited. Sir Topham Hatt leaned out of the window to wave to Edward and Henry, but the train was going so fast that his hat blew off into a field, where a goat ate it for his lunch.

They never stopped till they came to the Big Station at the end of the line.

The passengers all got out and said, "Thank you." And Sir Topham Hatt promised Henry a new coat of paint.

"Would you like blue and red?"

"Yes, please," said Henry. "Then I'll be like Edward."

Edward and Henry went home quietly, and on their way they helped Gordon back to the Shed.

All three engines are now great friends.

Wasn't Henry pleased when he had his new coat. He is very proud of it, as all good engines are—he doesn't mind the rain now, because he knows that the  best way to keep his paint nice is not to run into tunnels but to ask his Driver to rub him down when the day's work is over.

THE RAILWAY SERIES

SINCE 1945

Thomas the Tank Engine

Thomas the Tank Engine

THE REV. W. AWDRY

with illustrations by

C. REGINALD DALBY

DEAR CHRISTOPHER,

Here is your friend Thomas the Tank Engine. He wanted to come out of his station yard and see the world. These stories tell you how he did it.

I hope you will like them because you helped me to make them.

YOUR LOVING DADDY

Thomas and Gordon

Thomas was a tank engine who lived at the Big Station. He had six small wheels, a short stumpy funnel, a short stumpy boiler, and a short stumpy dome.

He was a fussy little engine, always pulling coaches about. He pulled them to the station ready for the big engines to take out on long journeys; and when trains came in and the people had got out, he would pull the empty coaches away so that the big engines could go and rest.

He was a cheeky little engine, too. He thought no engine

worked as hard as he did. So he
used to play tricks on them.
He liked best of all to come
quietly beside a big engine
dozing on a siding and
make him jump.

"*Peep, peep, peep, pip, peep!* Wake up, lazybones!" he
would whistle. "Why don't you work hard like me?"

Then he would laugh rudely and run away to find
some more coaches.

One day, Gordon was resting on a siding. He was very tired. The big Express he always pulled had been late, and he had had to run as fast as he could to make up for lost time.

He was just going to sleep when Thomas came up in his cheeky way.

"Wake up, lazybones," he whistled. "Do some hard work for a change—you can't catch me!" And he ran off laughing.

Instead of going to sleep again, Gordon thought how he could get Thomas back.

One morning, Thomas wouldn't wake up. His Driver and Fireman couldn't make him start. His fire went out, and there was not enough steam.

It was nearly time for the Express. The people were waiting, but the coaches weren't ready.

At last, Thomas started. "Oh, dear! Oh, dear!" he yawned.

"Come on," said the coaches. "Hurry up." Thomas gave them a rude bump and started for the station.

"Don't dawdle, don't dawdle," he grumbled.

"Where have you been? Where have you been?" asked the coaches crossly.

Thomas fussed into the station, where Gordon was waiting.

"*Poop, poop, poop.* Hurry up, you," said Gordon crossly.

"*Peep, pip, peep.* Hurry yourself," said cheeky Thomas.

"Yes," said Gordon, "I will." And almost before the coaches had stopped moving, Gordon came out of his siding and was coupled to the train.

"*Poop, poop,*" he whistled. "Get in quickly, please." So the people got in quickly, the signal went down, the clock struck the hour, the Guard waved his green flag, and Gordon was ready to start.

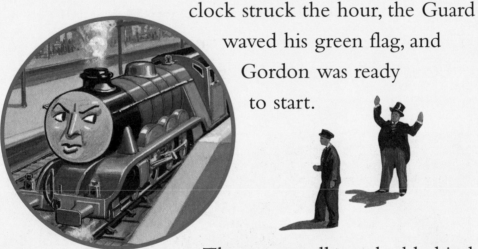

Thomas usually pushed behind the big trains to help them start. But he was always uncoupled first so that, when the train was running nicely, he could stop and go back.

This time, he was late, and Gordon started so quickly that they forgot to uncouple Thomas.

"Poop, poop," said Gordon.

"Peep, peep, peep," whistled Thomas.

"Come on! Come on!" puffed Gordon to the coaches.

"Pull harder! Pull harder!" puffed Thomas to Gordon.

The heavy train slowly began to move out of the station.

The train went faster and faster—too fast for Thomas. He wanted to stop, but he couldn't.

"Peep! Peep! Stop! Stop!" he whistled.

"Hurry, hurry, hurry," laughed Gordon in front.

"You can't get away. You can't get away," laughed the coaches.

Poor Thomas was going faster than he had ever gone before. He was out of breath and his wheels hurt him, but he had to go on.

"I shall never be the same again," he thought sadly. "My wheels will be quite worn out."

At last, they stopped at a station. Everyone laughed to see Thomas puffing and panting behind.

They uncoupled him, put him onto a turntable, and then he ran on a siding out of the way.

"Well, little Thomas," chuckled Gordon as he passed. "Now you know what hard work means, don't you?"

Poor Thomas couldn't answer. He had no breath. He just puffed slowly away to rest and had a long, long drink.

He went home very slowly and was careful afterwards never to be cheeky to Gordon again.

Thomas' Train

Thomas often grumbled because he was not allowed to pull passenger trains.

The other engines laughed. "You're too impatient," they said. "You'd be sure to leave something behind!"

"Rubbish," said Thomas crossly. "You just wait. I'll show you."

One night, he and Henry were alone. Henry was ill. The men worked hard, but he didn't get better.

Now, Henry usually pulled the first train in the morning, and Thomas had to get his coaches ready.

"If Henry is ill," he thought, "perhaps I shall pull his train."

Thomas ran to find the coaches.

"Come *along*. Come *along*," he fussed.

"There's plenty of time, there's plenty of time," grumbled the coaches.

He took them to the platform and wanted to run round in front at once. But his Driver wouldn't let him.

"Don't be impatient, Thomas," he said.

So Thomas waited and waited. The people got in, the Guard and the Station Master walked up and down, the porters banged the doors, and still Henry didn't come.

Thomas got more and more excited every minute.

Sir Topham Hatt came out of his office to see what was the matter, and the Guard and the Station Master told him about Henry.

"Find another engine," he ordered.

"There's only Thomas," they said.

"You'll have to do it then, Thomas. Be quick now!"

So Thomas ran round to the front and backed up to the coaches, ready to start.

"Don't be impatient," said his Driver. "Wait till everything is ready."

But Thomas was too excited to listen to a word he said.

What happened then, no one knows. Perhaps they forgot to couple Thomas to the train, perhaps Thomas was too impatient to wait till they were ready, or perhaps his Driver pulled the lever by mistake.

Anyhow, Thomas started. People shouted and waved at him, but he didn't stop.

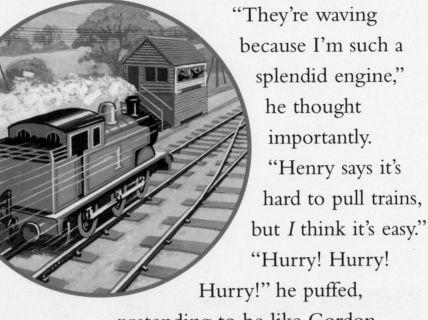

"They're waving because I'm such a splendid engine," he thought importantly. "Henry says it's hard to pull trains, but *I* think it's easy." "Hurry! Hurry! Hurry!" he puffed, pretending to be like Gordon.

As he passed the first signal box, he saw the men leaning out, waving and shouting.

"They're pleased to see me," he thought. "They've never seen *me* pulling a train before. It's nice of them to wave." And he whistled, "*Peep, peep,* thank you," and hurried on.

But he came to a signal—"Danger."

"Bother!" he thought. "I must stop, and I was going so nicely, too. What a nuisance signals are!" And he blew an angry *"peep, peep"* on his whistle.

One of the Signalmen ran up. "Hullo, Thomas!" he said. "What are you doing here?"

"I'm pulling a train," said Thomas proudly. "Can't you *see*?"

"Where are your coaches, then?"

Thomas looked back. "Why, bless me," he said, "if we haven't left them behind!"

"Yes," said the Signalman, "you'd better go back quickly and fetch them."

Poor Thomas was so sad he nearly cried.

"Cheer up!" said his Driver. "Let's go back quickly and try again."

At the station, all the passengers were talking at once. They were telling Sir Topham Hatt, the Station Master, and the Guard what a bad railway it was.

But when Thomas came back and they saw how sad he was, they couldn't be cross. So they coupled him to the train, and this time he *really* pulled it.

But for a long time afterwards the other engines laughed at Thomas and said:

"Look, there's Thomas, who wanted to pull a train but forgot about the coaches!"

Thomas and the Freight Cars

Thomas used to grumble in the Shed at night. "I'm tired of pushing coaches. I want to see the world."

The others didn't take much notice, for Thomas was a little engine who talked big.

But one night, Edward came to the Shed. He was a kind little engine and felt sorry for Thomas.

"I've got some freight cars to take home tomorrow," he told him. "If you take them instead, I'll push coaches in the Yard."

"Thank you," said Thomas, "that will be nice."

So they asked their Drivers the next morning, and when they said "Yes," Thomas ran happily to find the freight cars.

Now, freight cars are silly and noisy. They talk a lot and don't attend to what they are doing. They don't listen to their engine, and when he stops, they bump into each other, screaming,

"Oh! Oh! Oh! Oh! Whatever is happening?"

And, I'm sorry to say, they play tricks on an engine who is not used to them.

Edward knew all about freight cars. He warned Thomas to be careful, but Thomas was too excited to listen.

The Switchman fastened the coupling, and when the signal dropped, Thomas was ready.

The Guard blew his whistle. *"Peep! Peep!"* answered Thomas, and started off.

But the freight cars weren't ready.

"Oh! Oh! Oh! Oh!" they screamed as their couplings tightened. "Wait, Thomas, wait." But Thomas wouldn't wait.

"Come—on. Come—on," he puffed, and the freight cars grumbled slowly out of the siding onto the Main Line.

Thomas was happy. "Come along. Come along," he puffed.

"All—right!—Don't—fuss.—All—right!—Don't fuss," grumbled the freight cars. They clattered through stations and rumbled over bridges.

Thomas whistled, *"Peep! Peep!"* and they rushed through the tunnel in which Henry had been shut up.

Then they came to the top of the hill where Gordon had gotten stuck.

"Steady now, steady," warned the Driver, and he shut off steam and began to put on the brakes.

"We're stopping, we're stopping," called Thomas.

"No! No! No! No!" answered the freight cars, and bumped into each other. "Go—on!—Go—on!" And before his Driver could stop them, they had pushed Thomas down the hill, and were rattling and laughing behind him.

Poor Thomas tried hard to stop them from making him go too fast.

"Stop pushing, stop pushing," he hissed, but the freight cars would not stop.

"Go—on!—Go—on!" they giggled in their silly way.

He was glad when they got to the bottom. Then he saw the place where they had to stop.

"Oh, dear! What shall I do?"

They rattled through the station, and luckily the line was clear as they swerved into the Freight Yard.

"Oo————ooh e————r," groaned Thomas as his brakes held fast and he skidded along the rails.

"I must stop." And he shut his eyes tight.

When he opened them, he saw he had stopped just in front of the buffers, and there watching him was—Sir Topham Hatt!

"What are *you* doing here, Thomas?" he asked sternly.

"I've brought Edward's freight cars," Thomas answered.

"Why did you come so fast?"

"I didn't mean to. I was *pushed*," said Thomas sadly.

"Haven't you pulled freight cars before?"

"No."

"Then you've a lot to learn about freight cars, little Thomas. They are silly things and must be kept in their place. After pushing them about here for a few weeks, you'll know almost as much about them as Edward. Then you'll be a Really Useful Engine."

Thomas and the Breakdown Train

Every day, Sir Topham Hatt came to the station to catch his train, and he always said "Hullo" to Thomas.

There were lots of freight cars in the Yard—different ones came in every day—and Thomas had to push and pull them into their right places.

He worked hard—he knew now that he wasn't so clever as he had thought. Besides, Sir Topham Hatt had been kind to him, and he wanted to learn all about freight cars so he could be a Really Useful Engine.

But on a siding by themselves were some freight cars that Thomas was told he "mustn't touch."

There was a small coach, some flatbed trucks, and two queer things his Driver called cranes.

"That's the breakdown train," he said. "When there's an accident, the workmen get into the coach and the engine takes them quickly to help the hurt people and to clear and mend the line. The cranes are for lifting heavy things like engines and coaches and freight cars."

One day, Thomas was in the Yard when he heard an engine whistling, "Help! Help!" and a goods train came rushing through much too fast.

The engine (a new one called James) was frightened. His brake blocks were on fire, and smoke and sparks streamed out on each side.

"They're *pushing* me! They're *pushing* me!" he panted.

"On! On! On! On!" laughed the freight cars.

"Help! Help!" yelled poor James as he disappeared under a bridge.

"I'd like to teach those freight cars a lesson," said Thomas the Tank Engine.

Presently, a bell rang in the signal box, and a man came running. "James is off the line—the breakdown train—quickly!" he shouted.

So Thomas was coupled on, the workmen jumped into their coach, and off they went.

Thomas worked his hardest. "Hurry! Hurry! Hurry!" he puffed, and this time he wasn't pretending to be like Gordon—he really meant it.

"Bother those freight cars and their tricks," he thought. "I hope poor James isn't hurt."

They found James and the freight cars at a bend in the line. The brake van and the last few freight cars

were on the rails, but the front ones were piled in a heap; James was in a field with a cow looking at him, and his Driver and Fireman were feeling him all over to see if he was hurt.

"Never mind, James," they said. "It wasn't your fault. It was those wooden brakes they gave you. We always said they were no good."

Thomas pushed the breakdown train alongside. Then he pulled the unhurt freight cars out of the way.

"Oh—dear!—Oh—dear!" they groaned.

"Serves you right. Serves you right," puffed Thomas crossly.

When the men put other freight cars on the line, he pulled them away, too. He was hard at work, puffing backwards and forwards, all the afternoon.

"This'll teach you a lesson, this'll teach you a lesson," he told the freight cars, and they answered, "Yes—it—will.—Yes—it—will," in a sad, groany, creaky sort of voice.

They left the broken freight cars and mended the line. Then, with the two cranes, they put James back on the rails. He tried to move, but he couldn't, so Thomas helped him back to the Shed.

Sir Topham Hatt was waiting anxiously for them.

"Well, Thomas," he said kindly, "I've heard all about it, and I'm very pleased with you. You're a Really Useful Engine.

"James shall have some proper brakes and a new coat of paint, and you. . . shall have a Branch Line all to yourself."

"Oh, Sir!" said Thomas happily.

Now Thomas is as happy as can be. He has a Branch Line all to himself, and puffs proudly backwards and forwards with two coaches all day.

He is never lonely, because there is always some engine to talk to at the junction.

Edward and Henry stop quite often and tell him the news. Gordon is always in a hurry and does not stop, but he never forgets to say *"Poop, poop"* to little Thomas, and Thomas always whistles *"Peep, peep"* in return.

James the Red Engine

 James and the Top Hat

 James and the Bootlace

 Troublesome Trucks

 James and the Express

James the Red Engine

THE REV. W. AWDRY

with illustrations by

C. REGINALD DALBY

Dear Friends of Edward, Gordon, Henry, and Thomas,

Thank you for your kind letters. Here is the new book for which you asked.

James, who crashed into the story of *Thomas the Tank Engine,* settles down and becomes a Useful Engine.

We are nationalized now, but the same engines still work the Region. I am glad, too, to tell you that Sir Topham Hatt, who understands our friends' ways, is still in charge.

I hope you will enjoy this book, too.

The Author

James and the Top Hat

James was a new engine who lived at a station at the other end of the line. He had two small wheels in front and six driving wheels behind. They weren't as big as Gordon's, and they weren't as small as Thomas'.

"You're a special mixed-traffic engine," Sir Topham Hatt told him. "You'll be able to pull coaches or freight cars quite easily."

But freight cars are not easy things to manage, and on his first day they had pushed him down a hill into a field.

He had been ill after the accident, but now he had new brakes and a shining coat of red paint.

"The red paint will cheer you up after your accident," said Sir Topham Hatt kindly. "You are to pull coaches today, and Edward shall help you."

They went together to find the coaches.

"Be careful with the coaches, James," said Edward. "They don't like being bumped. Freight cars are silly and noisy—they need to be bumped and taught to behave—but coaches get cross and will get you back."

They took the coaches to the platform and were both coupled on in front. Sir Topham Hatt, the Station Master,

and some little boys all came to admire James' shining rods and red paint.

James was pleased. "I am a really splendid engine," he thought, and suddenly let off steam. *"Whee— ee—ee—ee—eesh!"*

Sir Topham Hatt, the Station Master, and the Guard all jumped, and a shower of water fell on Sir Topham Hatt's nice new top hat.

Just then the whistle blew, and James thought they had better go—so they went!

"Go on, go on," he puffed to Edward.

"Don't push, don't push," puffed Edward, for he did not like starting quickly.

"Don't go so fast, don't go so fast," grumbled the

coaches, but James did not listen. He wanted to run away before Sir Topham Hatt could call him back.

He didn't even want to stop at the first station. Edward tried hard to stop, but the two coaches in front were beyond the platform before they stopped, and they had to go back to let the passengers get out.

Lots of people came to look at James, and as no one seemed to know about Sir Topham Hatt's top hat, James felt happier.

Presently, they came to the junction where Thomas

was waiting with his two coaches.

"Hullo, James!" said Thomas kindly. "Feeling better? That's good. Ah! That's my Guard's whistle. I must go. Sorry I can't stay. I don't know what Sir Topham Hatt would do without me to run this Branch Line." And he puffed off importantly with his two coaches into a tunnel.

Leaving the junction, they passed the field where James had had his accident. The fence was mended, and the cows were back again. James whistled, but they paid no attention.

They clattered through Edward's station yard and started to climb the hill beyond.

"It's ever so steep, it's ever so steep," puffed James.

"I've done it before, I've done it before," puffed Edward.

"It's steep, but we'll do it—it's steep, but we'll do it," the two engines puffed together as they pulled the train up the big hill.

They both rested at the next station. Edward told James how Gordon had been stuck on the hill and he had had to push him up!

James laughed so much that he got hiccups and surprised an old lady in a black bonnet.

She dropped all her parcels, and three porters, the Station Master, and the Guard had to run after her, picking them up!

James was quiet in the Shed that night. He had enjoyed his day, but he was a little afraid of what Sir Topham Hatt would say about the top hat!

James and the Bootlace

Next morning, Sir Topham Hatt spoke severely to James: "If you can't behave, I shall take away your red coat and have you painted blue."

James did not like that at all, and he was very rough with the coaches as he brought them to the platform.

"Come along, come along," he called rudely.

"All in good time, all in good time," the coaches grumbled.

"Don't talk, come on!" answered James, and with the coaches squealing and grumbling after him, he snorted into the station.

James *was* cross that morning. Sir Topham Hatt had spoken to him, the coaches had dawdled, and worst of all, he had had to fetch his own coaches. "Gordon never does," thought James, "and he is only painted blue. A splendid red engine like me should never have to fetch his own coaches." And he puffed and snorted round to the front of the train and backed up to it with a rude bump.

"O—ooooh!" groaned the coaches. "That was so bad!"

To make James even crosser, he then had to take the coaches to a different platform, where no one came near him as he stood there. Sir Topham Hatt was in his office, the Station Master was at the other end of the train with the Guard, and even the little boys stood a long way off.

James felt lonely. "I'll show them!" he said to himself. "They think Gordon is the only engine who can pull coaches."

And as soon as the Guard's whistle blew, he started off with a tremendous jerk.

"Come on!—Come on!—Come on!" he puffed, and the coaches, squeaking and groaning in protest,

clattered over the switches onto the open line.

"Hurry!—Hurry!—Hurry!" puffed James.

"You're going too fast, you're going too fast," said the coaches, and indeed they were going so fast that they swayed from side to side.

James laughed and tried to go faster, but the coaches wouldn't let him.

"We're going to stop—we're going to stop—we're—going—to—stop," they said, and James found himself going slower and slower.

"What's the matter?" James asked his Driver.

"The brakes are on—leak in the pipe, most likely. You've banged the coaches enough to make a leak in anything."

The Guard and the Driver got down and looked at the brake pipes all along the train.

At last they found a hole where rough treatment had made a joint work loose.

"How shall we mend it?" said the Guard.

James' Driver thought for a moment.

"We'll do it with newspapers and a leather bootlace."

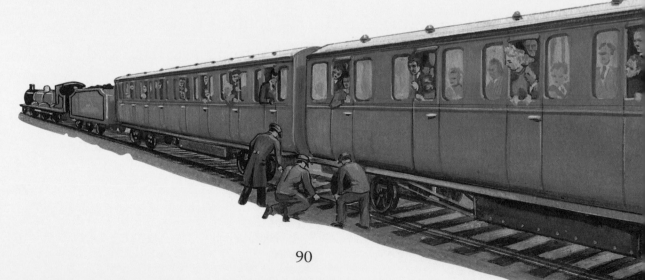

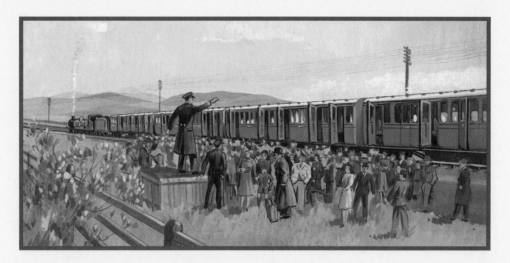

"Well, where is the bootlace coming from?" asked the Guard. "We haven't got one."

"Ask the passengers," said the Driver.

So the Guard made everyone get out.

"Has anybody got a leather bootlace?" he asked.

They all said "No," except one man in a bowler hat (whose name was Jeremiah Jobling) who tried to hide his feet.

"You have a leather bootlace there, I see, sir," said the Guard. "Please give it to me."

"I won't," said Jeremiah Jobling.

"Then," said the Guard sternly, "I'm afraid this train will just stay where it is."

Then the passengers all told the Guard, the Driver, and the Fireman what a bad railway it was. But the Guard climbed into his car, and the Driver and Fireman made James let off steam. So they all told Jeremiah Jobling he was a bad man instead.

At last, he gave them his laces, the Driver tied a pad

of newspapers tightly round the hole, and James was able to pull the train.

But he was a sadder and a wiser James, and took care never to bump coaches again.

Troublesome Trucks

James did not see Sir Topham Hatt for several days. They left James alone in the Shed, and did not even allow him to go out and push coaches and freight cars in the Yard.

"Oh, dear!" he thought sadly. "I'll never be allowed out anymore; I shall have to stay in this Shed for always, and no one will ever see my red coat again. Oh, dear! Oh, dear!" James began to cry.

Just then Sir Topham Hatt came along.

"I see you are sorry, James," he said. "I hope now that you will be a better engine. You have given me a lot of trouble. People are laughing at my railway, and I do not like that at all."

"I am very sorry, Sir," said James. "I will try hard to behave."

"That's a good engine," said Sir Topham Hatt kindly. "I want you to pull some freight cars for me. Run along and find them."

So James puffed happily away.

"Here are your freight cars, James," said a little tank engine. "Have you got some bootlaces ready?" And he ran off, laughing rudely.

"Oh! Oh! Oh!" said the freight cars as James backed up to them. "We want a proper engine, not a red monster."

James took no notice and started as soon as the Guard was ready.

"Come along, come along," he puffed.

"We won't! We won't!" screamed the freight cars.

But James didn't care, and he pulled the screeching freight cars sternly out of the Yard.

The freight cars tried hard to make him give up, but he still kept on.

Sometimes their brakes would slip on, and sometimes their axles would "run hot." Each time they would have to stop and put the trouble right, and each time James would start again, determined not to let the freight cars beat him.

"Give up! Give up! You can't pull us! You can't! You can't!" called the freight cars.

"I can and I will! I can and I will!" puffed James.

And slowly but surely, he pulled them along the line.

At last, they saw Gordon's hill ahead.

"Look out for trouble, James," warned his Driver. "We'll go fast and get them up before they know it. Don't let them stop you."

So James went faster, and they were soon halfway up the hill.

"I'm doing it! I'm doing it!" he panted.

But it was hard work.

"Will the top never come?" he thought, when with a sudden jerk it all came easier.

"I've done it! I've done it!" he puffed triumphantly.

"Hurrah!" he thought. "It's easy now." But his Driver shut off steam.

"They've done it again," he said. "We've left our tail behind!"

The last ten freight cars were running backwards down the hill. The coupling had snapped!

But the Guard was brave. Very carefully and cleverly he made them stop. Then he got out and walked down the line with his red flag.

"That's why it was easy," said James as he backed the other freight cars carefully down. "What silly things freight cars are! There might have been an accident."

Meanwhile, the Guard had stopped Edward, who was pulling three coaches.

"Shall I help you, James?" called Edward.

"No, thank you," answered James, "I'll pull them myself."

"Good. Don't let them beat you."

So James got ready. Then with a *"peep, peep,"* he was off.

"I *can* do it, I *can* do it," he puffed. He pulled and puffed as hard as he could.

"*Peep, pip, peep, peep!* You're doing well!" whistled Edward as James slowly struggled up the hill, with clouds of smoke and steam pouring from his funnel.

"I've done it, I've done it," he panted, and disappeared over the top.

They reached their station safely. James was resting in the Yard when Edward puffed by with a cheerful *"peep, peep."*

Then, walking towards him across the rails, James saw . . . Sir Topham Hatt!

"Oh, dear! What will he say?" he asked himself sadly.

But Sir Topham Hatt was smiling. "I was in Edward's train and saw everything," he said. "You've made the most troublesome freight cars on the line behave. After that, you deserve to keep your red coat."

James and the Express

Sometimes Gordon and Henry slept in James' Shed, and they would talk of nothing but bootlaces! James would talk about engines who got shut up in tunnels and stuck on hills, but they wouldn't listen and went on talking and laughing.

"You talk too much, little James," Gordon would say. "A fine strong engine like me has something to talk about. I'm the only engine who can pull the Express. When I'm not there, they need two engines. Think of that!"

"I've pulled expresses for years and have never once

lost my way. I seem to know the right line by instinct," said Gordon proudly. Every wise engine knows, of course, that the Signalman works the switches to make engines

run on the right lines, but Gordon was so proud that he had forgotten.

"Wake up, James," he said next morning. "It's nearly time for the Express. What are you doing? Odd jobs? Ah, well! We all have to begin somewhere, don't we? Run along now and get my coaches—don't be late now."

James went to get Gordon's coaches. They were now all shining with lovely new paint. He was careful not to bump them, and they followed him smoothly into the station, singing happily. "We're going away, we're going away."

"I wish I was going with you," said James. "I would love to pull the Express and go flying along the line."

He left them in the station and went back to the Yard just as Gordon, with much noise and blowing of steam, backed up to the train.

Sir Topham Hatt was on the train with other important people, and as soon as they heard the Guard's whistle, Gordon started.

"Look at me now! Look at me now!" he puffed, and the coaches glided after him out of the station.

"*Poop, poop, poo, poo, poop!*—Goodbye, little James! See you tomorrow."

James watched the train disappear round a curve and then went back to work. He pushed some freight cars into their proper sidings and went to fetch the coaches for another train.

He brought the coaches to the platform and was just being uncoupled when he heard a mournful, quiet *"Shush, shush, shush, shush!"* And there was Gordon, trying to sidle into the station without being noticed.

"Hullo, Gordon! Is it tomorrow?" asked James. Gordon didn't answer. He just let off steam feebly.

"Did you lose your way, Gordon?"

"No, it was lost for me," he answered crossly. "I was switched off the Main Line onto the loop. I had to go all round and back again."

"Perhaps it was instinct," said James brightly.

Meanwhile, all the passengers hurried to the ticket office. "We want our money back," they shouted.

Everyone was making noise, but Sir Topham Hatt climbed on a trolley and blew the Guard's whistle so loudly that they all stopped to look at him.

Then he promised them a new train at once.

"Gordon can't do it," he said. "Will you pull it for us, James?"

"Yes, Sir, I'll try."

So James was coupled on, and everyone got in again.

"Do your best, James," said Sir Topham Hatt kindly. Just then the whistle blew, and he had to run to get in.

"Come along, come along," puffed James.

"You're pulling us well! You're pulling us well," sang the coaches.

"Hurry, hurry, hurry," puffed James.

Stations and bridges flashed by, the passengers leaned out of the windows and cheered, and they soon reached the terminus.

Everyone said "Thank you" to James.

"Well done," said Sir Topham Hatt. "Would you like to pull the Express sometimes?"

"Yes, please," answered James happily.

The next day when James came by, Gordon was pushing freight cars in the Yard.

"I like some quiet work for a change," he said. "I'm teaching these freight cars manners. You did well with those coaches, I hear. . . . Good, we'll show them!" And he gave his freight cars a bump, making them cry, "Oh! Oh! Oh! Oh!"

James and Gordon are now good friends. James sometimes takes the Express to give Gordon a rest. Gordon never talks about bootlaces, and they are both quite agreed on the subject of freight cars!

Tank Engine Thomas Again

 Thomas and the Guard

 Thomas Goes Fishing

 Thomas, Terence, and the Snow

 Thomas and Bertie

Tank Engine Thomas Again

THE REV. W. AWDRY

with illustrations by

C. REGINALD DALBY

DEAR FRIENDS,

Here is news from Thomas' Branch Line. It is
clearly no ordinary line, and life on it is far from dull.

Thomas asks me to say that if you are ever in the
Region, you must be sure to visit him and travel on
his line. "They will have never seen anything like it,"
he says proudly.

I know I haven't!

THE AUTHOR

Thomas and the Guard

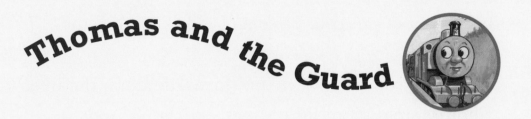

Thomas the Tank Engine is very proud of his Branch Line. He thinks it is the most important part of the whole railway.

He has two coaches. They are old and need new paint, but he loves them very much. He calls them Annie and Clarabel. Annie can only take passengers,

but Clarabel can take passengers, luggage, and the Guard.

As they run backwards and forwards along the line, Thomas sings them little songs, and Annie and Clarabel sing, too.

When Thomas starts from a station, he sings, "Oh, come along! We're rather late. Oh, come along! We're rather late." And the coaches sing, "We're coming along, we're coming along."

They don't mind what Thomas says to them

because they know he is trying to please Sir Topham Hatt. And they know that if Thomas is cross, he is not cross with them.

He is cross with the engines on the Main Line who have made him late.

One day, they had to wait for Henry's train. It was late. Thomas was getting crosser and crosser. "How can I run my line properly if Henry is always late? He doesn't realize that Sir Topham Hatt depends on ME." And he whistled impatiently.

At last, Henry came.

"Where have you been, lazybones?" asked Thomas crossly.

"Oh, dear, my system is out of order. No one understands my case. You don't know what I suffer," moaned Henry.

"Rubbish!" said Thomas. "You're too fat. You need exercise!"

Lots of people with piles of luggage got out of Henry's train, and they all climbed into Annie and Clarabel. Thomas had to wait till they were ready. At last, the Guard blew his whistle, and Thomas started at once.

The Guard turned round to jump into his car, tripped over an old lady's umbrella, and fell flat on his face.

By the time he had picked himself up, Thomas, Annie, and

Clarabel were steaming out of the station.

"Come along! Come along!" puffed Thomas, but Clarabel didn't want to come. "I've lost my nice Guard, I've lost my nice Guard," she sobbed. Annie tried to tell Thomas, "We haven't a Guard, we haven't

a Guard," but he was hurrying and wouldn't listen.

"Oh, come along! Oh, come along!" he puffed impatiently.

Annie and Clarabel tried to put on their brakes, but they couldn't without the Guard.

"Where is our Guard? Where is our Guard?" they cried. Thomas didn't stop till they came to a signal.

"Bother that signal!" said Thomas. "What's the matter?"

"I don't know," said his Driver. "The Guard will tell us in a minute." They waited and waited, but the Guard didn't come.

"*Peep, peep, peep, peep!* Where is the Guard?" whistled Thomas.

"We've left him behind," sobbed Annie and Clarabel together. The Driver, the Fireman, and the passengers looked, and there was the Guard, running as fast as he could along the line, with his flags in one hand and his whistle in the other.

Everybody cheered him.

He was very hot, so he sat down and had a drink and told them all about it.

"I'm very sorry, Mr. Guard," said Thomas.

"It wasn't your fault, Thomas. It was the old lady's umbrella. Look, the signal is down. Let's make up for lost time."

Annie and Clarabel were so pleased to have their Guard again that they sang, "As fast as you like, as fast as you like!" to Thomas all the way, and they reached the end of the line quicker than ever before.

Thomas Goes Fishing

Thomas' Branch Line had a station by a river. As he rumbled over the bridge, he would see people fishing. Sometimes they stood quietly by their lines, sometimes they were actually jerking fish out of the water.

Thomas often wanted
to stay and watch,
but his Driver said,
"No! What
would Sir
Topham Hatt say
if we were late?"
Thomas
thought it
would be

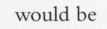

lovely to stop by
the river. "I would like to go fishing," he
said to himself longingly.

Every time he met another engine,
he would say, "I want to fish." They
all answered, "Engines don't go fishing."
"Silly stick-in-the-muds!" he would snort
impatiently.

Thomas generally had to take in water at the station
by the river. One day, he stopped as usual, and his
Fireman put the pipe from the water tower into his

tank. Then he turned the tap, but it was out of order and no water came.

"Bother!" said Thomas. "I am thirsty."

"Never mind," said his Driver. "We'll get some water from the river."

They found a bucket and some rope and went to the bridge. Then the Driver let the bucket down to the water.

The bucket was old and had five holes, so they had to fill it, pull it up, and empty it into Thomas' tank as quickly as they could.

"There's a hole in my bucket, dear Liza, dear Liza," sang the Fireman.

"Never mind about Liza," said the Driver. "You empty that bucket before you spill the water over me!"

They finished at last. "That's good! That's good!" puffed Thomas as he started, and Annie and Clarabel ran happily behind.

They puffed along the valley and were in the tunnel when Thomas began to feel a pain in his boiler. Steam hissed from his safety valve in an alarming way.

"There's too much steam," said his Driver, and his Fireman opened the tap in the feed pipe to let more water into the boiler, but none came.

"Oh, dear," groaned Thomas, "I'm going to burst! I'm going to burst!"

They damped down his fire and struggled on.

"I've got such a pain, I've got such a pain," Thomas hissed.

Just outside the last station, they stopped, uncoupled Annie and Clarabel, and ran Thomas, who was still hissing fit to burst, on a siding right out of the way.

Then, while the Guard telephoned for an Engine Inspector and the Fireman was putting out the fire, the Driver wrote notices in large letters, which he hung on Thomas in front and behind: DANGER! KEEP AWAY.

Soon the Inspector and Sir Topham Hatt arrived. "Cheer up, Thomas!" they said. "We'll soon make you right."

The Driver told them what had happened. "So the feed pipe is blocked," said the Inspector. "I'll just look in the tank."

He climbed up and peered in, then came down. "Excuse me, Sir," he said to Sir Topham Hatt, "please look in the tank and tell me what you see."

"Certainly, Inspector." He clambered up, looked in, and nearly fell off in surprise.

"Inspector," whispered Sir Topham Hatt, "can *you* see *fish*?"

"Gracious goodness me!" he said. "How did the fish get there, Driver?"

Thomas' Driver scratched his head. "We must have fished them from the river." And he told them about the bucket.

Sir Topham Hatt laughed. "Well, Thomas, so you and your Driver have been fishing. But fish don't suit you, and we must get them out."

So the Driver and the Fireman fetched rods and nets, and they all took turns at fishing in Thomas' tank while Sir Topham Hatt told them how to do it.

When they had caught all the fish, the Station Master gave them some potatoes, the Driver borrowed

a frying pan, and the Fireman made a fire beside the line and did the cooking.

Then they all had a lovely picnic supper of fish and chips.

"That was good," said Sir Topham Hatt as he finished his share. "But fish don't suit you, Thomas, so you mustn't do it again."

"No, Sir, I won't," said Thomas sadly. "Engines don't go fishing. It's too uncomfortable."

Thomas, Terence, and the Snow

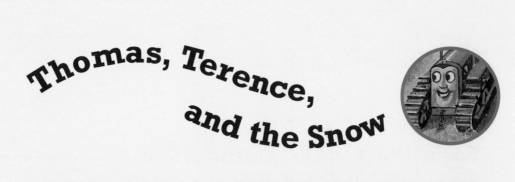

Autumn was changing the leaves from green to brown. The fields were changing, too, from yellow stubble to brown earth.

As Thomas puffed along, he heard the *"chug, chug, chug"* of a tractor at work.

One day, stopping for a signal, he saw the tractor close by.

"Hullo!" said the tractor. "I'm Terence; I'm plowing."

"I'm Thomas. I'm pushing a train. What ugly wheels you've got."

"They're not ugly, they're caterpillars," said Terence. "I can go anywhere; *I* don't need rails."

"I don't want to go *anywhere*," said Thomas huffily. "I like my rails, thank you!"

Thomas often saw Terence working, but though he whistled, Terence never answered.

Winter came, and with it dark, heavy clouds full of snow.

"I don't like it," said Thomas' Driver. "A heavy fall is coming. I hope it doesn't stop us."

"Pooh!" said Thomas, seeing the snow melt on the rails. "Soft stuff, nothing to it!" And he puffed on, feeling cold but confident.

They finished their journey safely, but the country was covered and the rails were two dark lines standing out in the white snow.

"You'll need your snowplow for the next journey, Thomas," said his Driver.

"Pooh! Snow is silly soft stuff—it won't stop me."

"Listen to me," his Driver replied. "We are going to put your snowplow on, and I want no nonsense, please."

The snowplow was heavy and uncomfortable, and made Thomas cross. He shook it and he banged it, and when they got back, it was so damaged that the Driver had to take it off.

"You're a very naughty engine," said his Driver as he shut the Shed door that night.

The next morning, both the Driver and the Fireman came early and worked hard to mend the snowplow, but they couldn't make it fit properly.

It was time for the first train. Thomas was pleased. "I don't have to wear it, I don't have to wear it," he puffed to Annie and Clarabel.

"I hope it's all right, I hope it's all right," they whispered anxiously to each other.

The Driver was anxious, too. "It's not bad here," he said to the Fireman, "but it's sure to be deep in the valley."

It was snowing again when Thomas started, but the rails were not covered.

"Silly soft stuff! Silly soft stuff!" he puffed. "I didn't need that stupid old thing yesterday. I don't today. Snow can't stop me." And he rushed into the tunnel, thinking how clever he was.

At the other end, he saw a heap of snow fallen from the sides of the cutting.

"Silly old snow," said Thomas, and charged it.

"Cinders and ashes!" said Thomas. "I'm stuck!" And he was!

"Back! Thomas, back!" said his Driver. Thomas tried, but his wheels spun and he couldn't move.

More snow fell and piled up round him.

The Guard went back for help while the Driver, Fireman, and passengers tried to dig the snow away. But as fast as they dug, more snow slipped down, until Thomas was nearly buried.

"Oh, my wheels and coupling rods!" said Thomas sadly. "I shall have to stop here till I'm frozen. What a silly engine I am." And Thomas began to cry.

At last, a tooting in the distance told them a bus

had come for the passengers.

Then Terence chugged through the tunnel.

He pulled the empty coaches away and came back for Thomas. Thomas' wheels were clear, but still spun helplessly when he tried to move.

Terence tugged and slipped, and slipped and tugged, and at last dragged Thomas into the tunnel.

"Thank you, Terence. Your caterpillars are splendid," said Thomas gratefully.

"I hope you'll be sensible now, Thomas," said his Driver severely.

"I'll try," said Thomas as he puffed home.

Thomas and Bertie

O ne day, Thomas was waiting at the junction when a bus came into the Yard.

"Hullo!" said Thomas. "Who are you?"

"I'm Bertie. Who are you?"

"I'm Thomas. I run this line."

"So you're Thomas. Ah—I remember now. You got stuck in the snow, I took your passengers, and Terence

pulled you out. I've come to help you with your passengers today."

"Help me!" said Thomas crossly, going bluer than ever and letting off steam. "I can go faster than you."

"You can't."

"I can."

"I'll race you," said Bertie.

Their Drivers agreed. The Station Master said, "Are you ready?—Go!" And they were off.

Thomas never could go fast at first, and Bertie drew in front. Thomas was running well, but he did not hurry.

"Why don't you go fast? Why don't you go fast?" called Annie and Clarabel anxiously.

"Wait and see, wait and see," hissed Thomas.

"He's a long way ahead, a long way ahead," they wailed, but Thomas didn't mind. He remembered the crossing.

There was Bertie fuming at the gates while they sailed gaily through.

"Goodbye, Bertie," called Thomas.

The road left the railway and went through a village, so they couldn't see Bertie.

They stopped at the station. "*Peep, pip, peep!* Quickly, please!" called Thomas. Everybody got out quickly, the Guard whistled, and off they went.

"Come along! Come along!" sang Thomas.

"We're coming along! We're coming along!" sang Annie and Clarabel.

"Hurry! Hurry! Hurry!" panted Thomas, looking straight ahead.

Then he whistled shrilly in horror, for Bertie was crossing the bridge over the railway, tooting triumphantly on his horn!

"Oh, deary me! Oh, deary me!" groaned Thomas.

"He's a long way in front, a long way in front," wailed Annie and Clarabel.

"Steady, Thomas," said his Driver, "we'll beat Bertie yet."

"We'll beat Bertie yet, we'll beat Bertie yet," echoed Annie and Clarabel.

"We'll do it, we'll do it," panted Thomas bravely. "Oh, bother, there's a station."

As he stopped, he heard a toot.

"Goodbye, Thomas, you must be tired. Sorry I can't stop—we buses have to work, you know. Goodbye!"

The next station was by the river. They got there quickly, but the signal was up.

"Oh, dear," thought Thomas, "we've lost!"

But he felt better after a drink.

Then James rattled through with a goods train, and the signal dropped, showing the line was clear.

"Hurrah, we're off! Hurrah, we're off!" puffed Thomas gaily.

As they rumbled over the bridge, they heard an impatient *"Toot, toot,"* and there was Bertie waiting at the red light while cars and trucks crossed the narrow bridge in the opposite direction.

Road and railway ran up the valley side by side, a stream tumbling between.

Thomas had not crossed the bridge when Bertie started with a roar—and soon shot ahead. Excited passengers in the train and the bus cheered and shouted across the valley. Now Thomas reached his full speed, and foot by foot, yard by yard, he gained,

till they were running level. Bertie tried hard, but Thomas was too fast. Slowly but surely, he drew ahead, till whistling triumphantly, he plunged into the tunnel, leaving Bertie toiling far behind.

"I've done it! I've done it," panted Thomas in the tunnel.

"We've done it, hooray! We've done it, hooray!" chanted Annie and Clarabel. Whistling proudly, they *whooooshed* out of the tunnel into the last station.

The passengers gave Thomas three cheers and told the Station Master and the porters all about the race. When Bertie came in, they gave him three cheers, too.

"Well done, Thomas," said Bertie. "That was fun, but to beat you over that hill I would have to grow wings and be an airplane."

Thomas and Bertie now keep each other very busy. Bertie finds people in the villages who want to go by train and takes them to Thomas, while Thomas brings people to the station for Bertie to take home.

They often talk about their race. But Bertie's passengers don't like being bounced like peas in a frying pan! And Sir Topham Hatt has warned Thomas about what happens to engines who race at dangerous speeds.

So although (between you and me) they would like to have another race, I don't think they ever will.

THE RAILWAY SERIES

SINCE 1945

1

Troublesome Engines

 Henry and the Elephant

 Tenders and Turntables

 Trouble in the Shed

 Percy Runs Away

Troublesome Engines

THE REV. W. AWDRY

with illustrations by

C. REGINALD DALBY

DEAR FRIENDS,

   News from the Main Line has not been good.
Sir Topham Hatt has been having trouble. A short
while ago, he gave Henry a coat of green paint, but
as soon as he got his old color back again, Henry
became conceited. Gordon and James, too, have
been getting above themselves.

   I am glad to say, however, that Sir Topham Hatt
has, quite kindly but very firmly, put them in their
place. And now the trains are running as usual.

   I hope you will like meeting Percy. We shall be
hearing more of him later.

                                        THE AUTHOR

Henry and the Elephant

Henry and Gordon were lonely when Thomas left the Yard to run his Branch Line. They missed him very much.

They had more work to do. They couldn't wait in the Shed till it was time and find their coaches at the

platform—they had to fetch them. They didn't like that.

Edward sometimes did odd jobs, and so did James, but James soon started grumbling, too. Sir Topham Hatt kindly gave Henry and Gordon new coats of paint (Henry chose green), but they still grumbled dreadfully.

"We get no rest, we get no rest," they complained as they clanked about the Yard.

But the coaches only laughed. "You're lazy and slack, you're lazy and slack," they answered in their quiet, rude way.

But when a circus came to town, the engines forgot

they were tired. They all wanted to shunt the special freight cars and coaches.

They were dreadfully jealous of James when Sir Topham Hatt told him to pull the train when the circus went away.

However, they soon forgot about the animals as they had plenty of work to do.

One morning, Henry was told to take some workmen to a tunnel that was blocked.

He grumbled away to find two freight cars to carry the workmen and their tools.

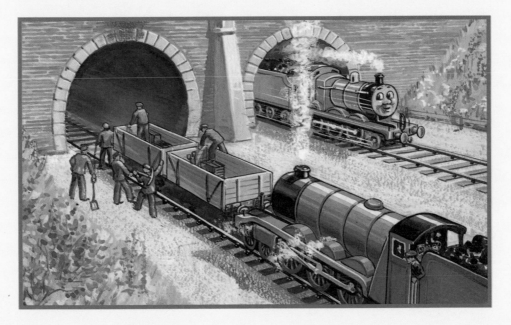

"Pushing freight cars! Pushing freight cars!" he muttered in a sulky sort of way.

They stopped outside the tunnel and tried to look through it, but it was quite dark; no daylight shined from the other end.

The workmen took their tools and went inside. Suddenly—with a shout—they all ran out, looking frightened.

"We went to the block and started to dig, but it grunted and moved," they said.

"Rubbish," said the Foreman.

"It's not rubbish, it's big and alive; we're not going in there again."

"Right," said the Foreman, "I'll ride in a freight car, and Henry will push it out."

"*Wheeeesh,*" said Henry unhappily. He hated tunnels (he had been shut up in one once), but this was worse; something big and alive was inside.

"*Peep, peep, peep, pip, pip, pee—eep!*" he whistled. "I don't want to go in!"

"Neither do I," said his Driver, "but we must clear the line."

"Oh, dear! Oh, dear!" puffed Henry as they slowly advanced into the darkness.

B U M P————!!!!

Henry's Driver shut off steam at once.

"Help! Help! We're going back," wailed Henry. And slowly moving out into the daylight came first Henry, then the freight cars, and last of all, pushing hard and rather cross, came a large elephant.

"Well, I never!" said the Foreman. "It's an elephant from the circus."

Henry's Driver put on his brakes, and a man ran to telephone for the keeper.

The elephant stopped pushing and came towards them. They gave him some sandwiches and cake, so he forgot he was cross and remembered he was hungry. He drank three buckets of water without stopping, and was just going to drink another when Henry let off steam.

The elephant jumped and—"*hoo———oosh*"—he

squirted the water over Henry by mistake.

Poor Henry!

When the keeper came, the workmen rode home happily in the freight cars, laughing at their adventure, but Henry was very cross.

"An elephant pushed me! An elephant *hoosh*ed me!" he hissed.

He was sulky all day, and his coaches had an uncomfortable time.

In the Shed, Henry told Gordon and James about the elephant. And I am sorry to say that instead of laughing and telling him not to be silly, they looked sad and said, "You poor engine, you have been badly treated."

Tenders and Turntables

The big stations at both ends of the line each have a turntable. Sir Topham Hatt had them made so that Edward, Henry, Gordon, and James can be turned round. It is dangerous for tender engines to go fast backwards. Tank engines like Thomas don't need turntables; they can go just as well backwards as forwards.

But if you had heard Gordon talking a short while ago, you would have thought that Sir Topham Hatt had given him a tender just to show how important he was.

"You don't understand, little Thomas," said Gordon. "We tender engines have a position to keep up. You haven't a tender, and that makes a difference. It doesn't matter where *you* go, but *we* are *important,* and for Sir Topham Hatt to make us shunt freight cars, fetch coaches, and go on some of those dirty sidings, it's—

it's—well, it's not the *proper thing*."

And Gordon puffed away in a dignified manner.

Thomas chuckled and went off with Annie and Clarabel.

When he arrived at the terminus, Gordon waited till all the passengers got out. Then, groaning and grumbling, he shunted the coaches to another platform.

"Disgraceful! Disgraceful!" he hissed as he ran backwards to the turntable.

The turntable was in a windy place close to the sea. It was only just big enough for Gordon. And if he was not on it just right, he put it out of balance and made it difficult to turn.

Today, Gordon was in a bad temper and the wind was blowing fiercely.

His Driver tried to make him stop in the right place;

backward and forward they went, but Gordon wasn't trying.

At last, Gordon's Driver gave it up. The Fireman tried to turn the handle, but Gordon's weight and the strong wind prevented him. The Driver, some platelayers, and the Fireman all tried together.

"It's no good," they said at last, mopping their faces. "Your tender upsets the balance. If you were a nice tank engine, you'd be all right. Now, you'll have to pull the next train backwards."

Gordon came to the platform. Some little boys shouted, "Come on quick, here's a new tank engine."

"What a swiz!" they said when they came near. "It's only Gordon back to front."

Gordon hissed emotionally.

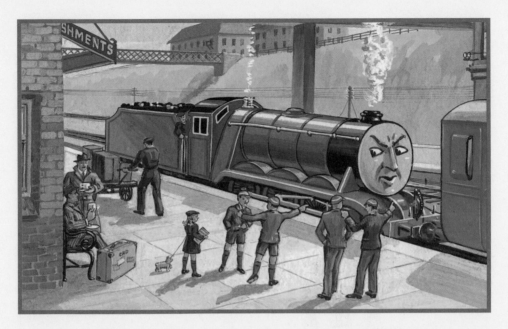

He puffed to the junction. "Hullo!" called Thomas. "Playing tank engines? Sensible engine! Take my advice, scrap your tender and have a nice bunker instead."

Gordon snorted but didn't answer. Even James laughed when he saw him. "Take care," hissed Gordon, "you might stick, too."

"No fear," chuckled James, "I'm not so fat as you."

"I mustn't stick," thought James anxiously as he ran to the turntable later. He stopped on just the right place to balance the table. It could now swing easily.

His Fireman turned the handle . . . James turned . . . much too easily! The wind puffed him round like a top. He couldn't stop . . . !

At last, the wind died down, and James stopped turning, but not before Gordon, who had been turned on the loop line, had seen him.

"Well! Well!" he said. "Are you playing roundabouts?"

Poor James, feeling quite giddy, rolled off to the Shed without a word.

That night, Henry, Gordon, and James had an "indignation meeting."

"It's shameful to treat tender engines like this! Henry gets *hoosh*ed by elephants. Gordon has to go backwards and people think he's a tank engine. James spins round like a top. And everyone laughs at us. And added to that, Sir Topham Hatt makes us shunt in dirty sidings. Ugh!!" said all three engines together.

"Listen," said Gordon. He whispered something to the others. "We'll do it tomorrow. Sir Topham Hatt *will* look silly!"

Trouble in the Shed

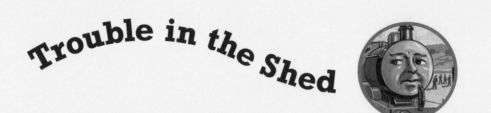

S ir Topham Hatt sat in his office and listened. Sir
Topham Hatt frowned and said, "What a nuisance
passengers are! How can I work with all this noise?"

The Station Master knocked and came in, looking
worried.

"There's trouble in the Shed, Sir. Henry is sulking; there is no train, and the passengers are saying this is a bad railway."

"Indeed!" said Sir Topham Hatt. "We cannot allow that. Will you calm the passengers, please; I will go and speak to Henry."

He found Henry, Gordon, and James looking sulky.

"Come along, Henry," he said, "it is time your train was ready."

"Henry's not going," said Gordon rudely. "We *won't* shunt like *common* tank engines. We are *important*

tender engines. You fetch our coaches and we will pull them. Tender engines don't shunt." And all three engines let off steam in a cheeky way.

"Oh, indeed," said Sir Topham Hatt severely. "We'll see about that; engines on *my* railway do as they are told."

He hurried away, climbed into his car, and drove to find Edward.

"The Yard has never been the same since Thomas left," he thought sadly.

Edward was shunting.

"Leave those trucks, please, Edward; I want you to push coaches for me in the Yard."

"Thank you, Sir, that will be a nice change."

"That's a good engine," said Sir Topham Hatt kindly. "Off you go then."

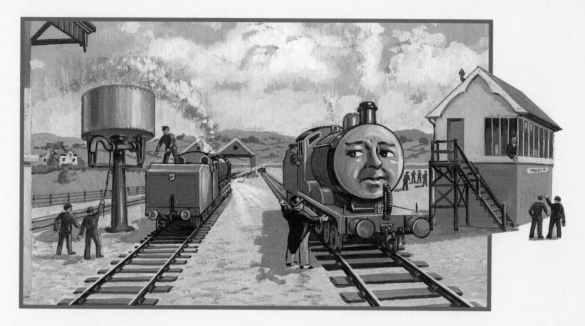

So Edward found coaches for the three engines, and that day the trains ran as usual.

But when Sir Topham Hatt came the next morning, Edward looked unhappy.

Gordon came clanking past, hissing rudely. "Bless me!" said Sir Topham Hatt. "What a noise!"

"They all hiss me, Sir," answered Edward sadly. "They say, 'Tender engines don't shunt,' and last night they said I had black wheels. I haven't, have I, Sir?"

"No, Edward, you have nice blue ones, and I'm proud of you. Tender engines do shunt, but all the

same, you'd be happier in your own yard. We need a tank engine here."

He went to an Engine Workshop, and the workmen showed him all sorts of tank engines. There were big ones and little ones; some looked happy and some sad, and some looked at him anxiously, hoping he would choose them.

At last, he saw a smart little green engine with four wheels.

"That's the one," he thought.

"If I choose you, will you work hard?"

"Oh, Sir! Yes, Sir!"

"That's a good engine; I'll call you Percy."

"Yes, Sir! Thank you, Sir!" said Percy happily.

So he bought Percy and drove him back to the Yard.

"Edward," he called, "here's Percy; will you show him everything?"

Percy soon learned what he had to do, and they had a happy afternoon.

Once, Henry came by hissing as usual.

"Whee———eesh!" said Percy suddenly. Henry jumped and ran back to the Shed.

"How beautifully you *wheesh*ed him," laughed Edward. "I can't *wheesh* like that."

"Oh!" said Percy modestly. "That's nothing. You should hear them in the Workshop. You have to *wheesh* loudly to make yourself heard."

Next morning, Thomas arrived. "Sir Topham Hatt sent for me; I expect he wants help," he said importantly to Edward.

"Shh! Shh! Here he comes."

"Well done, Thomas; you've been quick. Listen, Henry, Gordon, and James are sulking; they say they won't shunt like common tank engines. So I have shut them up, and I want you both to run the line."

"Common tank engines indeed!" snorted Thomas. "We'll show them."

"And Percy here will help, too," said Sir Topham Hatt.

"Oh, Sir! Yes, Sir! Please, Sir!" answered Percy excitedly.

Edward and Thomas worked the line. Starting at opposite ends, they pulled the trains, whistling cheerfully to each other as they passed.

Percy sometimes puffed along the Branch Line. Thomas was anxious, but both the Driver and Guard promised to take care of Annie and Clarabel.

There were fewer trains, but the passengers didn't mind. They knew the three other engines were having a lesson.

Henry, Gordon, and James stayed shut in the Shed, and were cold, lonely, and miserable. They wished now they hadn't been so silly.

Percy Runs Away

Henry, Gordon, and James were shut up for several days. At last, Sir Topham Hatt opened the Shed.

"I hope you are sorry," he said sternly, "and understand you are not so important after all. Thomas, Edward, and Percy have worked the line very nicely. They need a change, and I will let you out if you promise to be good."

"Yes, Sir!" said the three engines. "We will."

"That's right, but please remember that this 'no shunting' nonsense must stop."

He told Edward, Thomas, and Percy that they could go and play on the Branch Line for a few days.

They ran off happily and found Annie and Clarabel at the junction. The two coaches were so pleased to see Thomas again, and he took them for a run at once. Edward and Percy played with freight cars.

"Stop! Stop! Stop!" screamed the freight cars as they

were pushed into their proper sidings. But the two engines laughed and went on shunting till the freight cars were neatly arranged.

Next, Edward took some empty freight cars to the Quarry, and Percy was left alone.

Percy didn't mind that a bit. He liked watching trains and being cheeky to the engines.

"Hurry! Hurry! Hurry!" he would call to them. Gordon, Henry, and James got very cross!

After a while, he took some freight cars over the

Main Line to another siding. When they were nice
and neat, he ran onto the Main Line again and waited
for the Signalman to set the switches so that he could
cross back to the Yard.

Edward had warned Percy, "Be careful on the Main
Line. Whistle to tell the Signalman you are there."

But Percy didn't remember to whistle, and the
Signalman was so busy that
he forgot about Percy.

Bells rang in the
signal box. The
Signalman
answered, saying
the line was clear,
and set the signals
for the next train.

Percy waited and
waited, but the switches
were still against him. He looked
along the Main Line. Rushing straight toward him
was Gordon with the Express.

"Peep! Peep!" Percy whistled in horror.

"Poop, poop, poo-poo-poop!" whistled Gordon.

His Driver shut off the steam and applied the brakes.

Percy's Driver turned on full steam. "Back, Percy! Back!" he urged, but Percy's wheels wouldn't turn quickly. Gordon was coming so fast that it seemed he couldn't stop. With eyes shut, Percy waited for the crash. His Driver and Fireman jumped out.

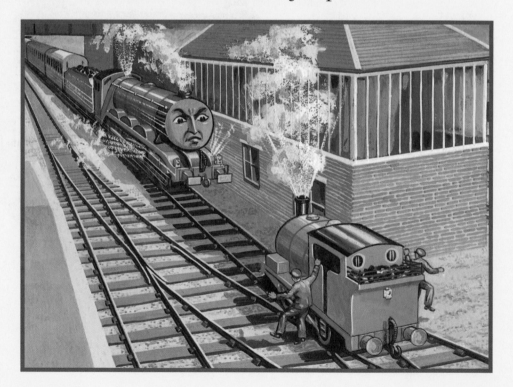

"Oo——ooh e——er!" groaned Gordon. "Get out of my way."

Percy opened his eyes. Gordon had stopped with Percy's buffers a few inches from his own.

But Percy had begun to move. "I—won't—stay—here—I'll—run—a—way," he puffed. He was soon clear of the station and running as fast as he could. He went through Edward's station, whistling loudly, and was so frightened that he ran right up Gordon's Hill without stopping.

He was tired then and wanted to stop, but he

couldn't—he had no Driver to shut off the steam or to apply the brakes.

"I shall have to run till my wheels wear out," he thought sadly. "Oh, dear! Oh, dear!"

"I—want—to—stop—I—want—to—stop," he puffed in a tired sort of way.

He passed another signal box. "I know just what you want, little Percy," called the Signalman kindly. He set the switches, and Percy puffed wearily onto a nice empty siding, ending in a big mound of earth.

Percy was too tired now to care where he went. "I—want—to—stop—I—want—to—stop————I—*have*—stopped!" he puffed thankfully as his bunker buried itself in the mound.

"Never mind, Percy," said the workmen as they dug him out. "You shall have a drink and some coal, and then you'll feel better."

Presently Gordon arrived. "Well done, Percy. You started so quickly that you stopped a nasty accident."

"I'm sorry I was cheeky," said Percy. "You were

clever to stop."

Percy now works in the Yard and finds coaches for the trains. He is still cheeky because he is that sort of engine, but he is always *most* careful when he goes on the Main Line.

Henry the Green Engine

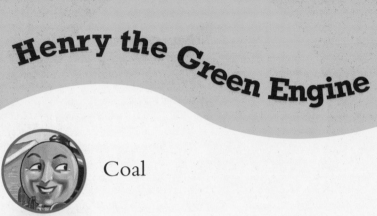 Coal

 The Flying Kipper

 Gordon's Whistle

 Percy and the Trousers

Henry's Sneeze

Henry the Green Engine

THE REV. W. AWDRY
with illustrations by
C. REGINALD DALBY

DEAR FRIENDS,

Here is more news from the Region. All the engines now have numbers as well as names; you will see them in the pictures. They are as follows: THOMAS 1, EDWARD 2, HENRY 3, GORDON 4, JAMES 5, PERCY 6.

I expect you were sorry for Henry, who was often ill and unable to work. He gave Sir Topham Hatt a lot of worry. Now Henry has a new shape and is ready for anything. These stories tell you all about it.

THE AUTHOR

Coal

"I suffer dreadfully, and no one cares."

"Rubbish, Henry," snorted James, "you don't work hard enough."

Henry was bigger than James but smaller than Gordon. Sometimes he could pull trains; sometimes he had no strength at all.

Sir Topham Hatt spoke to him, too. "You are too expensive, Henry. You have had lots of new parts and new paint, too, but they've done you no good. If we can't make you better, we must get another engine instead of you."

This made Henry, his Driver, and his Fireman very sad.

Sir Topham Hatt was waiting when Henry came to the platform. He had taken off his hat and coat and put on overalls.

He climbed to the footplate, and Henry started.

"Henry is a bad steamer," said the Fireman. "I build up his fire, but it doesn't give enough heat."

Henry tried very hard, but it was no good. He didn't have enough steam, and they stopped outside Edward's station.

"Oh, dear!" thought Henry sadly. "I shall have to go away."

Edward took charge of the train. Henry stayed behind.

"What do you think is wrong, Fireman?" asked Sir Topham Hatt.

The Fireman mopped his face. "Excuse me, Sir," he answered, "but the coal is wrong. We've had a poor lot lately, and today it's worse. The other engines can manage; they have big fireboxes. Henry's is small and can't make the heat. With Welsh coal he'd be a different engine."

"It's expensive," said Sir Topham Hatt thoughtfully,

"but Henry must have a fair chance. James shall go and fetch some."

When the Welsh coal came, Henry's Driver and Fireman were excited.

"Now we'll show them, Henry, old fellow!" They carefully oiled all his joints and polished his brass till it shined like gold.

His fire had already been lit, so the Fireman "made" it carefully.

He put large lumps of coal like a wall round the outside. Then he covered the glowing middle part with smaller lumps.

"You're spoiling my fire," complained Henry.

"Wait and see," said the Fireman. "We'll have a roaring fire just when we want it."

He was right. When Henry reached the platform, the water was boiling nicely, and he had to let off steam to show how happy he was. He made such a noise that Sir Topham Hatt came out to see him.

"How are you, Henry?"

"Pip, peep, peep!" whistled Henry, "I feel fine!"

"Have you a good fire, Driver?"

"Never better, Sir, *and* plenty of steam."

"No record breaking," warned Sir Topham Hatt, smiling. "Don't push him too hard."

"Henry won't need pushing, Sir; I'll have to hold him back."

Henry had a lovely day. He had never felt so well in his life. He wanted to go fast, but his Driver wouldn't let him. "Steady, old fellow," he would say, "there's plenty of time."

They arrived early at the junction.

"Where have you been, lazybones?" asked Henry when Thomas puffed in. "I can't wait for dawdling tank engines like you! Goodbye!"

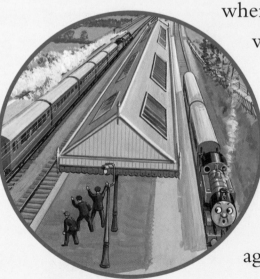

"*Whoooosh!*" said Thomas to Annie and Clarabel as Henry disappeared. "Have you ever seen anything like it?"

Both Annie and Clarabel agreed that they never had.

The Flying Kipper

Lots of ships use the harbor at the Big Station by the sea. The passenger ships have spotless paint and shining brass. Other ships, though smaller and dirtier, are important, too. They take coal, machinery, and other things abroad, and bring back meat, timber, and things we need.

Fishing boats also come there. They unload their

fish on the wharf. Some of it is sent to shops in the town, and some goes in a special train to other places far away.

The railwaymen call this train the "Flying Kipper."

One winter evening, Henry's Driver said, "We'll be out early tomorrow. We've got to take the Flying Kipper. Don't tell Gordon," he whispered, "but I think if we pull the Kipper nicely, Sir Topham Hatt will let us pull the Express."

"Hurrah!" cried Henry, excited. "That will be lovely."

He was ready at five o'clock. There was snow and frost. Men hustled and shouted, loading the cars with crates of fish. The last door banged, the Guard showed his green lamp, and they were off.

"Come on! Come on! Don't be silly! Don't be silly!" puffed Henry to the cars as his wheels slipped on the icy rails.

The cars shuddered and groaned. "*Trock, trick, trock, trick;* all right, all right," they answered grudgingly.

"That is better, that is better," puffed Henry more happily as the train began to gather speed.

Thick clouds of smoke and steam poured from his funnel into the cold air, and when his Fireman put on more coal, the fire's light shined brightly on the snow round.

"Hurry, hurry, hurry," panted Henry.

They *whoosh*ed under bridges and clattered through stations, green signal lights showing as they passed.

They were going well, the light grew better, and a yellow signal appeared ahead.

"Distant signal—up," thought Henry. "Caution." His Driver, shutting off steam, prepared to stop, but the home signal was down. "All clear, Henry; away we go."

They couldn't know the switches from the Main Line to a siding were frozen and that that signal had been set to "danger." A fall of snow had forced it down.

A freight train waited in the siding to let the Flying Kipper pass. The Driver and Fireman were drinking cocoa in the brake car.

The Guard pulled out his watch. "The Kipper is due," he said.

"Who cares?" said the Fireman. "This is good cocoa."

The Driver got up. "Come on, Fireman, back to our engine."

"Hey!" the Fireman grumbled. "I haven't finished my cocoa yet."

A sudden crash—the brake car broke—the three men shot in the air like jack-in-the-boxes and landed

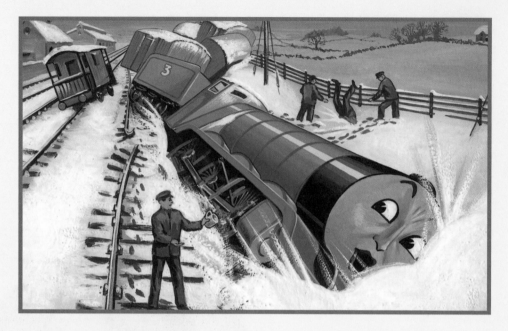

in the snow outside.

Henry's Driver and the Fireman jumped clear before the crash. The Fireman fell headfirst into a heap of snow. He kicked so hard that the Driver couldn't pull him out.

Henry sprawled on his side. He looked surprised. The freight train's Fireman waved his empty mug.

"You clumsy great engine! The best cup of cocoa I've ever had, and you bump into me and spill it all!"

"Never mind your cocoa, Fireman," laughed his Driver. "Run and telephone the breakdown gang."

The gang soon cleared the line, but they had hard work lifting Henry to the rails.

Sir Topham Hatt came to see him.

"The signal was down, Sir," said Henry nervously.

"Cheer up, Henry! It wasn't your fault. Ice and snow caused the accident. I'm sending you to Crewe, a fine place for sick engines. They'll give you a new shape and a larger firebox. Then you'll feel like a different engine and won't need special coal anymore.

Won't that be nice?"

"Yes, Sir," said Henry doubtfully.

Henry liked being at Crewe, but was glad to come home.

A crowd of people waited to see him arrive in his new shape. He looked so splendid and strong that they gave him three cheers.

"*Peep, peep, pippippeep!* Thank you very much," he whistled happily.

I am sorry to say that a lot of little boys are often late for school because they wait to see Henry go by!

They often see him pulling the Express, and he does it so well that Gordon is jealous. But that is another story.

Gordon's Whistle

G ordon was cross.

"Why should Henry have a new shape?" he grumbled. "A shape good enough for *me* is good enough for him. He goes gallivanting off to Crewe, leaving us to do his work. It's disgraceful!"

"And there's another thing. Henry whistles too much.

No *respectable* engine ever whistles loudly at stations.

"It isn't wrong," said Gordon, "but we just don't do it."

Poor Henry didn't feel happy anymore.

"Never mind," whispered Percy. "I'm glad you are home again. I like your whistling."

"Goodbye, Henry," called Gordon the next morning as he left the Shed. "We are glad to have you with us again, but be sure and remember what I said about whistling."

Later on, Henry took a slow train and presently stopped at Edward's station.

"Hullo, Henry," said Edward. "You look splendid. I was pleased to hear your happy whistle yesterday."

"Thank you, Edward," smiled Henry . . . "Shh! Shh! Can you hear something?"

Edward listened. Far away, but getting louder and louder, was the sound of an engine's whistle.

"It sounds like Gordon," said Edward, "and it ought to be Gordon, but Gordon never whistles like that."

But it *was* Gordon.

He came rushing down the hill at a tremendous rate. He didn't look at Henry, and he didn't look at Edward; he was purple in the boiler and whistling fit to burst.

He screamed through the station and disappeared.

"Well!!!" said Edward, looking at Henry.

"It isn't wrong," chuckled Henry, "but we just don't do it." And he told Edward what Gordon had said.

Meanwhile, Gordon screeched along the line. People came out of their houses, air raid sirens started, five fire departments got ready to go out, horses upset their carts, and old ladies dropped their parcels.

At the Big Station, the noise was awful. Porters and passengers held their ears. Sir Topham Hatt held his ears, too. He gave a lot of orders, but no one could hear them, and Gordon went on whistling. At last, he clambered into Gordon's cab.

"Take him away!" he bellowed. "AND STOP THAT NOISE!"

Still whistling, Gordon puffed sadly away.

He whistled as he crossed the switches; he whistled on the siding; he was still whistling as the last deafened passenger left the station.

Then two fitters climbed up and knocked his whistle valve into place————and there was *silence*.

Gordon slunk into the Shed. He was glad it was empty.

The others came in later. "It isn't wrong," murmured Henry to no one in particular, "but we just don't do it."

No one mentioned whistles!

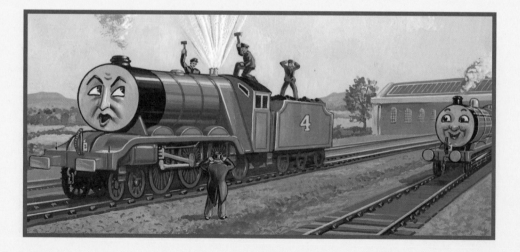

Percy and the Trousers

On cold mornings, Percy often saw workmen wearing scarves.

"My funnel's cold, my funnel's cold!" he would puff. "I want a scarf, I want a scarf."

"Rubbish, Percy," said Henry one day. "Engines don't want scarves!"

"Engines with proper funnels do," said Percy in his

cheeky way. "You've only got a small one!" Henry snorted; he was proud of his short, neat funnel.

Just then a train came in, and Percy, still puffing, "I want a scarf, I want a scarf," went to take the coaches to their siding.

His Driver always shut off steam just outside the station, and Percy would try to surprise the coaches by coming in as quietly as he could.

Two porters were taking some luggage across the line. They had a big load and were walking backwards to make sure that nothing fell.

Percy arrived so quietly that the porters didn't hear him till the trolley was on the line. The porters jumped clear. The trolley disappeared with a crunch.

Boxes and bags burst in all directions.

"Oo——ooh e——r!" groaned Percy, and stopped.

Sticky streams of red and yellow jam trickled down his face. A top hat hung on his lamp iron. Clothes, hats, boots, shoes, skirts, and blouses stuck to his front. A pair of striped trousers coiled lovingly round his funnel. They were gray no longer!

Angry passengers looked at their broken luggage. Sir Topham Hatt seized the top hat.

"Mine!" he said crossly.

"Percy," he shouted, "look at this!"

"Yes, Sir, I am, Sir," a muffled voice replied.

"My best trousers, too!"

"Yes, Sir, please, Sir," said Percy nervously.

"I am very cross," said Sir Topham Hatt. "We must pay the passengers for their spoiled clothes. My hat is dented, and my trousers are ruined, all because *you* come into the station as if you were playing hide-and-seek with the coaches."

The Driver unwound the trousers.

Sir Topham Hatt waved them away.

"Percy wanted a scarf. He shall have my trousers for a scarf. They will keep him warm."

Percy wore them back to the Yard.

He doesn't like scarves now!

This story is adapted from one told by Mr. C. Hamilton Ellis in *The Trains We Loved*. We gratefully acknowledge his permission to use it.

Henry's Sneeze

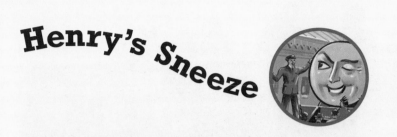

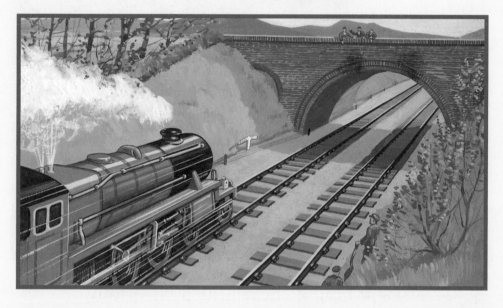

One lovely Saturday morning, Henry was puffing along. The sun shined, the fields were green, and the birds sang. Henry had plenty of steam in his boiler, and he was feeling happy.

"I feel so well, I feel so well," he sang.

"Trickety trock, trickety trock," hummed his coaches.

Henry saw some boys on a bridge.

"*Peep! Peep!* Hullo!" he whistled cheerfully.

"*Oh! Oh! Oooh!*" he called the next moment. For the boys didn't wave and take his number, but dropped stones on him instead.

They were silly, stupid boys who thought it would be fun to drop stones down his funnel. Some of the stones hit Henry's boiler and spoiled his paint, one hit the Fireman on the head as he was shoveling coal, and others broke the carriage windows.

"It's a shame, it's a shame," hissed Henry.

"They've broken our glass, they've broken our glass," sobbed the coaches.

The Driver opened the first-aid box, bandaged the Fireman's head, and planned what he was going to do.

They stopped the train, and the Guard asked if any passengers were hurt. No one was hurt, but everyone was cross. They saw the Fireman's bumped head and

213

told him what to do for it, and they looked at Henry's paint.

"Call the police," they shouted angrily.

"No!" said the Driver. "Leave it to Henry and me. We'll teach those boys a lesson."

"What will you do?" they asked.

"Can you keep a secret?" asked the Driver.

"Yes, yes," they all said.

"Well, then," said the Driver, "Henry is going to sneeze at them."

"What!" cried all the passengers.

The Driver laughed. "Henry draws air in through his fire and puffs it out with smoke and steam. When he puffs hard, the air blows ashes from his fire into his smokebox, and these ashes sometimes prevent him from puffing properly.

"When your nose is blocked, you sometimes sneeze. If Henry's smokebox is blocked, I can make air and

steam blow the ashes out through his funnel. We will do it at the bridge and startle those boys."

Henry puffed on to the terminus, where he had a rest.

Then he took the train back. Lots of people were waiting at the station just before the bridge. They wanted to see what would happen.

"Henry has plenty of ashes," said the Driver. "Please keep all windows shut till we have passed the bridge. Henry is as excited as we are, aren't you, old fellow?" And he patted Henry's boiler.

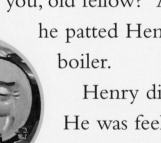

Henry didn't answer.

He was feeling stuffed up, but he winked at his Driver, like this.

The Guard's flag waved, his whistle blew, and they were off. Soon, in the distance, they saw the bridge. There were the boys, and they all had stones.

"Are you ready, Henry?" asked his Driver. "Sneeze hard when I tell you."

"NOW!" he said, and turned the handle.

"Atisha—Atisha—Atishooooh!"

Smoke and steam and ashes spouted from Henry's funnel. They went all over the bridge and all over the boys, who ran away as black as soot.

"Well done, Henry," laughed his Driver. "They won't drop stones on engines again."

"Your coat is all black, but we'll rub you down and paint your scratches, and you'll be as good as new tomorrow."

Henry has never again sneezed under a bridge. Sir Topham Hatt doesn't like it. His smokebox is always cleaned in the Yard while he is resting.

He has now gone under more bridges than he can count, but from that day to this, there have been no more boys with stones.

Toby the Tram Engine

Toby the Tram Engine

THE REV. W. AWDRY

with illustrations by

C. REGINALD DALBY

DEAR FRIENDS,

    Poor Thomas has been in trouble. So Sir Topham Hatt asked Toby to come and help run the Branch Line. Thomas and Toby are very good friends.

    Toby is a funny little engine with a queer shape. He works very hard and we are fond of him. We hope you will like him, too.

THE AUTHOR

Toby and the Stout Gentleman

Toby is a tram engine. He is short and sturdy. He has cowcatchers and side plates and doesn't look like a steam engine at all. He takes freight cars from farms and factories to the Main Line, and the big engines take them to London and elsewhere. His tram line runs along roads and through fields and

villages. Toby rings his bell cheerfully to everyone he meets.

He has a coach called Henrietta, who has seen better days. She complains because she has few passengers. Toby is attached to Henrietta and always takes her with him.

"She might be useful one day," he says.

"It's not fair at all!" grumbles Henrietta as the buses roar past full of passengers. She remembers that she used to be full, and nine freight cars would rattle

behind her.

Now there are only three or four, for the farms and factories send their goods mostly in trucks.

Toby is always careful on the road. The cars, buses, and trucks often have accidents. Toby hasn't had an accident for years, but the buses are crowded and Henrietta is empty.

"I can't understand it," says Toby the Tram Engine.

People come to see Toby, but they come by bus. They stare at him. "Isn't he quaint!" they say, and laugh.

They make him so cross.

One day, a car stopped close by, and a little boy jumped out. "Come on, Bridget," he called to his sister, and together they ran across to Toby. Two ladies and a stout gentleman followed. The gentleman looked important, but nice.

The children ran back. "Come on, Grandfather. Do look at this engine." And seizing his hands, they almost dragged him along.

"That's a tram engine, Stephen," said the stout gentleman.

"Is it electric?" asked Bridget.

"Whoosh!" hissed Toby crossly.

"Shh, shh!" said her brother. "You've offended him."

"But trams *are* electric, aren't they?"

"They are mostly," the stout gentleman answered, "but this is a steam tram."

"May we go in it, Grandfather? Please!"

The Guard had begun to blow his whistle.

"Stop," said the stout gentleman, and raised his hand. The Guard, surprised, opened his mouth, and the whistle fell out.

While he was picking it up, they all scrambled into Henrietta.

"Hip, hip, hurray!" chanted Henrietta, and she rattled happily behind.

Toby did not sing. "Electric indeed! Electric indeed," he snorted. He was very hurt.

The stout gentleman and his family got out at the junction, but waited for Toby to take them back to their car.

"What is your name?" asked the stout gentleman.

"Toby, sir."

"Thank you, Toby, for a very nice ride."

"Thank *you,* sir," said Toby politely. He felt better

now. "This gentleman," he thought, "is a gentleman who knows how to speak to engines."

The children came every day for a fortnight. Sometimes they rode with the Guard, sometimes in empty freight cars. On the last day of all, the Driver invited them into his cab.

All were sorry when they had to go away.

Stephen and Bridget said "Thank you" to Toby, his Driver, his Fireman, and the Guard.

The stout gentleman gave them all presents.

"*Peep, pip, pip, peep,*" whistled Toby. "Come

again soon."

"We will, we will," called the children, and they waved till Toby was out of sight.

The months passed. Toby had few freight cars and fewer passengers.

"Our last day, Toby," said his Driver sadly one morning. "The Manager says we must close tomorrow."

That day Henrietta had more passengers than she could manage. They rode in the freight cars and crowded in the brake van, and the Guard hadn't enough tickets to go round.

The passengers joked and sang, but Toby and his Driver wished they wouldn't.

"Goodbye, Toby," said the passengers afterwards. "We are sorry your line is closing down."

"So am I," said Toby sadly.

The last passenger left the station, and Toby puffed slowly to his shed.

"Nobody wants me," he thought, and went unhappily to sleep.

Next morning, the shed was flung open, and he

woke with a start to see his Fireman dancing a jig outside. His Driver, excited, waved a piece of paper.

"Wake up, Toby," they shouted, "and listen to this; it's a letter from the stout gentleman."

Toby listened and . . .

But I mustn't tell you any more, or I should spoil the next story.

Thomas in Trouble

There is a line to a quarry at the end of Thomas'
Branch; it goes for some distance along the road.

Thomas was always very careful here in case anyone
was coming.

"Peep, pip, peep!" he whistled; then the people got
out of the way, and he puffed slowly along with his
freight cars rumbling behind him.

Early one morning, there was no one on the road, but a large policeman was sitting on the grass close to the line. He was shaking a stone from his boot.

Thomas liked policemen. He had been a great friend of the Constable who used to live in the village, but he had just retired.

Thomas expected that the new Constable would be friendly, too.

"Peep, peep," he whistled. "Good morning."

The policeman jumped and dropped his boot.

He scrambled up and hopped round on one leg till he was facing Thomas.

Thomas was sorry to see that he didn't look friendly at all. He was red in the face and very cross.

The policeman wobbled about, trying to keep his balance.

"Disgraceful!" he spluttered. "I didn't sleep a wink last night. It was so quiet, and now engines come whistling suddenly behind me! My first day in the country, too!"

He picked up his boot and hopped over to Thomas.

"I'm sorry, sir," said Thomas. "I only said 'Good morning.'"

The policeman grunted and, leaning against Thomas' buffer, he put his boot on.

He drew himself up and pointed to Thomas.

"Where's your cowcatcher?" he asked accusingly.

"But I don't catch cows, sir!"

"Don't be funny!" snapped the policeman. He looked at Thomas' wheels. "No side plates, either." And he wrote in his notebook.

"Engines going on public roads must have their wheels covered and a cowcatcher in front. You haven't, so you are dangerous to the public."

"Rubbish!" said his Driver. "We've been along here

hundreds of times and never had an accident."

"That makes it worse," the policeman answered. He wrote "regular lawbreaker" in his book.

Thomas puffed sadly away.

Sir Topham Hatt was having breakfast. He was eating toast and marmalade. He had the newspaper open in front of him, and his wife had just given him some more coffee.

The butler knocked and came in.

"Excuse me, Sir, you are wanted on the telephone."

"Bother that telephone!" said Sir Topham Hatt.

"I'm sorry, my dear," he said a few minutes later. "Thomas is in trouble with the police, and I must go at once."

He gulped down his coffee and hurried from the room.

At the junction, Thomas' Driver told Sir Topham Hatt what had happened.

"Dangerous to the public indeed; we'll see about that!" And he climbed grimly into Annie the coach.

The policeman was at the other end of the platform. Sir Topham Hatt spoke to him at once, and a crowd collected to listen.

Other policemen came to see what was happening,

and Sir Topham Hatt argued with them, too, but it was no good.

"The law is the law," they said, "and we can't change it."

Sir Topham Hatt felt exhausted.

He mopped his face.

"I'm sorry, Driver," he said. "It's no use arguing with policemen. We will have to make those cowcatcher things for Thomas, I suppose."

"Everyone will laugh, Sir," said Thomas sadly. "They'll say I look like a tram."

Sir Topham Hatt stared, then he laughed.

"Well done, Thomas! Why didn't I think of it before? We want a tram engine! When I was on my holiday, I met a nice little engine called Toby. He hasn't enough work to do and needs a change. I'll write to his Controller at once."

A few days later, Toby arrived.

"That's a good engine," said Sir Topham Hatt. "I see you've brought Henrietta."

"You don't mind, do you, Sir?" asked Toby anxiously. "The Station Master wanted to use her as a henhouse, and that would never do."

"No, indeed," said Sir Topham Hatt gravely. "We couldn't allow that."

Toby made the freight cars behave even better than
Thomas did.

At first, Thomas was jealous, but he was so pleased
when Toby rang his bell and made the policeman
jump that they have been firm friends ever since.

Dirty Objects

Toby and Henrietta take the workmen to the Quarry every morning. At the junction they often meet James.

Toby and Henrietta were shabby when they first came and needed new paint. James was very rude. "Ugh! What *dirty* objects!" he would say.

At last, Toby lost patience.

"James," he asked, "why are you red?"

"I am a splendid engine," answered James loftily, "ready for anything. You never see *my* paint dirty."

"Oh!" said Toby innocently. "That's why you once needed bootlaces—to be ready, I suppose."

James went redder than ever and snorted off.

At the end of the line, James left his coaches and got ready for his next train. It was a "slow goods," stopping at every station to pick up and set down freight cars. James hated slow goods trains.

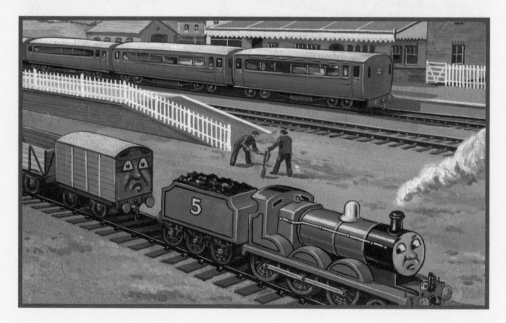

"Dirty freight cars from dirty sidings! Ugh!" he grumbled.

Starting with only a few, he picked up more and more freight cars at each station, till he had a long train. At first, the freight cars behaved well, but James bumped them so crossly that they decided to pay him back.

Presently, rumbling over the viaduct, they approached the top of Gordon's Hill. Heavy goods trains halt here to "pin down" their brakes. James had had an accident

with freight cars before and should have remembered this.

"Wait, James, wait," said his Driver, but James wouldn't wait. He was too busy thinking what he would say to Toby when they next met.

Too late he saw where he was and tried to stop.

"Hurrah! Hurrah!" laughed the freight cars, and banging their buffers, they pushed him down the hill.

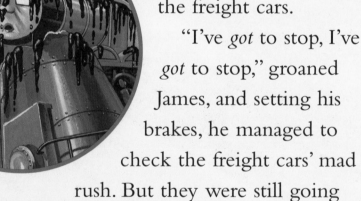

The Guard tightened his brakes until they screamed.

"On! On! On!" yelled the freight cars.

"I've *got* to stop, I've *got* to stop," groaned James, and setting his brakes, he managed to check the freight cars' mad rush. But they were still going much too fast to stop in time.

Through the station they thundered and lurched into the Yard.

James shut his eyes———

There was a bursting crash, and something sticky splashed all over him. He had run into two tar wagons and was black from smokebox to cab.

James was more dirty than hurt, but the tar wagons and some of the freight cars were broken. The breakdown train was in the Yard, and they soon tidied up the mess.

Toby and Percy were sent to help and came as quickly as they could.

"Look here, Percy!" exclaimed Toby. "Whatever is

that dirty object?"

"That's James; didn't you know?"

"It's James' shape," said Toby thoughtfully. "But James is a splendid red engine, and you never see *his* paint dirty."

James shut his eyes and pretended he hadn't heard.

They cleared away the unhurt freight cars and helped James home.

Sir Topham Hatt met them.

"Well done, Percy and Toby," he said.

He turned to James. "Fancy letting your freight cars run away. I *am* surprised. You're not fit to be seen; you must be cleaned at once.

"Toby shall have a coat of paint—chocolate and blue, I think."

"Please, Sir, can Henrietta have one, too?"

"Certainly, Toby," he smiled. "She shall have brown like Annie and Clarabel."

"Oh, thank you, Sir! She will be pleased."

Toby ran home happily to tell her the news.

Mrs. Kyndley's Christmas

It was nearly Christmas. Annie and Clarabel were packed full of people and parcels.

Thomas was having very hard work.

"Come on! Come on!" he puffed.

"We're feeling *so* full!" grumbled the coaches.

Thomas looked at the hill ahead. "Can I do it? Can I do it?" he puffed anxiously.

Suddenly, he saw a handkerchief waving from a cottage window. He felt better at once.

"Yes, I can, yes, I can," he puffed bravely. He pulled his

hardest and was soon through the tunnel and resting in the station.

"That was Mrs. Kyndley who waved to you, Thomas," his Driver told him. "She has to stay in bed all day."

"Poor lady," said Thomas. "I am sorry for her."

Engines have heavy loads at Christmastime, but

Thomas and Toby didn't mind the hard work when they saw Mrs. Kyndley waving.

But then it began to rain. It rained for days and days. Thomas didn't like it, nor did his Driver.

"Off we go, Thomas!" he would say. "Pull hard and get home quickly; Mrs. Kyndley won't wave today."

But whether she waved or not, they always whistled when they passed the little lonely cottage. Its white walls stood out against the dark background of the hills.

"Hullo!" exclaimed Thomas' Fireman one day. "Look at that!"

The Driver came across the cab. "Something's wrong there," he said.

Hanging, flapping and bedraggled, from a window of the cottage was something that looked like a large red flag.

"Mrs. Kyndley needs help, I expect," said the Driver, and put on the brakes. Thomas gently stopped.

The Guard came squelching through the rain up to Thomas' cab, and the Driver pointed to the flag.

"See if a doctor's on the train and ask him to go to the cottage; then walk back to the station and tell them we've stopped."

The Fireman went to see if the line was clear in front.

Two passengers left the train and climbed to the cottage. Then the Fireman returned.

"We'll back down to the station," said the Driver, "so that Thomas can get a good start."

"We shan't get up the hill," the Fireman answered. "Come and see what's happened!"

They walked along the line round the bend.

"Jiminy Christmas!" exclaimed the Driver. "Go back to the train; I'm going to the cottage."

He found the doctor with Mrs. Kyndley.

"Silly of me to faint," she said.

"You saw the red dressing gown? You're all safe?" asked Mrs. Kyndley.

"Yes," smiled the Driver. "I've come to thank you. There was a landslide in the cutting, doctor, and Mrs. Kyndley saw it from her window and stopped us. She's saved our lives!"

"God bless you, ma'am," said the Driver, and tiptoed from the room.

They cleared the line by Christmas Day, and the sun shined as a special train puffed up from the junction.

First came Toby, then Thomas with Annie and Clarabel, and last of all, but very pleased at being

allowed to come, was Henrietta.

Sir Topham Hatt was there, and lots of other people who wanted to say "Thank you" to Mrs. Kyndley.

"*Peepeep, peepeep!* Happy Christmas!" whistled the engines as they reached the place.

The people got out and climbed to the cottage. Thomas and Toby wished they could go, too.

Mrs. Kyndley's husband met them at the door.

Sir Topham Hatt and Thomas' Driver, Fireman, and Guard went upstairs, while the others stood in the

sunshine below the window.

The Driver gave her a new dressing gown to replace the one spoiled by the rain. The Guard brought her some grapes, and the Fireman gave her some woolly slippers and promised to bring some coal as a present from Thomas next time they passed.

Mrs. Kyndley was very pleased with her presents.

"You are very good to me," she said.

"The passengers and I," said Sir Topham Hatt, "hope you will accept these tickets for the South Coast,

Mrs. Kyndley, and get really well in the sunshine. We cannot thank you enough for preventing that accident. I hope we have not tired you. Goodbye and a happy Christmas."

Then going quietly downstairs, they joined the group outside the window and sang some carols before returning to the train.

Mrs. Kyndley is now at Bournemouth, getting better every day, and Thomas and Toby are looking forward to the time when they can welcome her home.

THE RAILWAY SERIES

SINCE 1945

Gordon the Big Engine

Gordon the Big Engine

THE REV. W. AWDRY

with illustrations by

C. REGINALD DALBY

DEAR IAN,

You asked for a book about Gordon. Here it is. Gordon has been naughty, and Sir Topham Hatt was stern with him.

Gordon has now learned his lesson and is a Really Useful Engine again.

THE AUTHOR

Off the Rails

Gordon was resting in a siding.

"*Peep, peep! Peep, peep!* Hullo, Fatface!" whistled Henry.

"What cheek!" spluttered Gordon. "That Henry is too big for his wheels; fancy speaking to me like that! Me-e-e-e!" he went on, letting off steam. "Me-e-e-e who has never had an accident!"

"Aren't jammed whistles and burst safety valves accidents?" asked Percy innocently.

"No, indeed!" said Gordon huffily. "High spirits— might happen to any engine; but to come off the rails, well, I ask you! Is it right? Is it decent?"

A few days later, it was Henry's turn to take the Express. Gordon watched him getting ready.

"Be careful, Henry," he said. "You're not pulling the Flying Kipper now; mind you keep on the rails today."

Henry snorted away. Gordon yawned and went to sleep.

But he didn't sleep long. "Wake up, Gordon," said his Driver. "A Special Train's coming and we're to pull it."

Gordon opened his eyes. "Is it coaches or freight?"

"Freight," said his Driver.

"Freight!" said Gordon crossly. *"Pah!"*

They lit Gordon's fire and oiled him ready for the run. The fire was sulky and wouldn't burn, but they couldn't wait, so Edward pushed him to the turntable to get him facing the right way.

"I *won't* go, I *won't* go," grumbled Gordon.

"Don't be silly, don't be silly," puffed Edward.

Gordon tried hard, but he couldn't stop himself being moved.

At last, he was on the turntable, Edward was uncoupled and backed away, and Gordon's Driver and Fireman jumped down to turn him round.

The movement had shaken Gordon's fire; it was now burning nicely and making steam.

Gordon was cross and didn't care what he did.

He waited till the table was halfway round. "I'll show them! I'll show them!" he hissed, and moved slowly forward.

He only meant to go a little way, just far enough to jam the table and stop it turning, as he had done once

before. But he couldn't stop himself and, slithering down the embankment, he settled in a ditch.

"*Oooosh!*" he hissed as his wheels churned the mud. "Get me out! Get me out!"

"Not a hope," said his Driver and Fireman. "You're stuck, you silly great engine. Don't you understand that?"

They telephoned Sir Topham Hatt.

"So Gordon didn't want to take the Special and ran into a ditch," he answered from his office. "What's that you say? The Special's waiting—tell Edward to take it, please—and Gordon? Oh, leave him where he is; we haven't time to bother with him now."

A family of toads croaked crossly at Gordon as he lay in the mud. On the other side of the ditch, some little boys were chattering.

"Gee! Doesn't he look silly!"

"They'll never get him out."

They began to sing:

Silly old Gordon fell in a ditch,
   fell in a ditch,
   fell in a ditch.
Silly old Gordon fell in a ditch,
  all on a Monday morning.

The school bell rang and, still singing, they ran down the road.

"Pshaw!" said Gordon, and blew away three tadpoles and an inquisitive newt.

Gordon lay in the ditch all day.

"Oh, dear!" he thought. "I shall never get out."

But that evening they brought floodlights; then with powerful jacks they lifted Gordon and made a road of sleepers under his wheels to keep him from the mud.

Strong wire ropes were fastened to his back end, and James and Henry, pulling hard, at last managed to bring him to the rails.

Late that night, Gordon crawled home a sadder and a wiser engine!

Leaves

Two men were cleaning Gordon.

"Mind my eye," Gordon grumbled.

"Shut it, silly! Did ever you see such mud, Bert?"

"No, I never, Alf! You ought to be ashamed, Gordon, giving us extra work."

The hosing and scrubbing stopped. Gordon opened one eye, but shut it quickly.

"Wake up, Gordon," said Sir Topham Hatt sternly, "and listen to me. You will pull no more coaches till you are a Really Useful Engine."

So Gordon had to spend his time pulling freight cars.

"Goods trains, goods trains," he muttered. He felt his position deeply.

"That's for you!—and *you*!—*and* you!" Gordon said

crossly.

"Oh! Oh! Oh! Oh!" screamed the freight cars as he shunted them about the Yard.

"Freight cars will be freight cars," said James, watching him.

"They won't with *me*!" snorted Gordon. "I'll teach them. Go on!" And another freight car scurried away.

"They tried to push me down the hill this morning," Gordon explained. "It's slippery there. You'll

probably need some help."

"*I* don't need help on hills," said James huffily.

Gordon laughed and got ready for his next train. James went away to take the Express.

"Slippery hills indeed," he snorted. "*I* don't need help."

"Come on! Come on!" he puffed.

"All in good time, all in good time," grumbled the coaches.

The train was soon running nicely, but a "distant" signal checked them close to Gordon's Hill.

Gordon's Hill used to be bleak and bare. Strong winds from the sea made it hard to climb. Trees were planted to give shelter, and in summer the trains run through a leafy avenue.

Now autumn had come, and dead leaves fell. The wind usually puffed them away, but today rain made

them heavy, and they did not move.

The "home" signal showed "clear," and James began to go faster.

He started to climb the hill.

"I'll do it! I'll do it!" he puffed confidently.

Halfway up he was not so sure! "I *must* do it, I *must* do it," he panted desperately. But try as he would, his wheels slipped on the leaves, and he couldn't pull the train at all.

"Whatsthematter? Whatsthematter?" he gasped.

"Steady, old boy, steady," soothed his Driver.

His Fireman put sand on the rails to help him grip,

but James' wheels spun so fast that they only ground the sand and leaves to slippery mud, making things worse than before.

The train slowly stopped. Then—

"Help! Help! Help!" whistled James, for though his wheels were turning forward, the heavy coaches pulled him backwards, and the whole train started slipping down the hill.

His Driver shut off steam, carefully put on the brakes, and skillfully stopped the train.

"Whew!" He sat down and mopped his face. "I've never known *that* to happen before."

"I have," said the Fireman, "in Bincombe Tunnel—Southern Region."

The Guard poked his head in the cab. "Now what?" he asked.

"Back to the station," said the Fireman, taking charge, "and send for a 'banker.'"

So the Guard warned the Signalman, and they brought the train safely down.

But Gordon, who had followed with a goods train, saw what had happened.

Gordon left his freight cars and crossed over to James.

"I thought you could climb hills," he chuckled.

James didn't answer; he had no steam!

"Ah, well! We live and learn," said Gordon. "We live and learn. Never mind, little James," he went on kindly. "I'm going to push behind. Whistle when you're ready."

James waited till he had plenty of steam, then *"Peep! Peep!"* he called.

"Poop! Poop! Poop! Pull hard," puffed Gordon.

"We'll do it!" puffed James.

"Pull hard! We'll do it," the engines puffed together.

Clouds of smoke and steam towered from the snorting engines as they struggled up the hill.

"We *can* do it!" puffed James.

"We *will* do it!" puffed

Gordon.

The greasy rails sometimes made Gordon's wheels slip, but he never gave up, and presently they reached the top.

"We've done it! We've done it!" they puffed.

Gordon stopped. *"Poop! Poop!"* he whistled. "Goodbye."

"*Peep! Peep! Peep! Peep!* Thank you! Goodbye," answered James. Gordon watched the coaches wistfully till they were out of sight, then slowly he trundled back to his waiting freight cars.

Down the Mine

One day, Thomas was at the junction when
Gordon shuffled in with some freight cars.

"*Poof!*" remarked Thomas. "What a funny smell!"

"Can you smell a smell?"

"I can't smell a smell," said Annie and Clarabel.

"A funny, musty sort of smell," said Thomas.

"No one noticed it till you did," grunted Gordon.

"It must be yours."

"Annie! Clarabel! Do you know what I think it is?" whispered Thomas loudly. "It's ditchwater!"

Gordon snorted, but before he could answer, Thomas puffed quickly away.

Annie and Clarabel could hardly believe their ears!

"He's *dreadfully* rude; I feel *quite* ashamed. I feel quite ashamed, he's dreadfully rude," they twittered to each other.

"You mustn't be rude; you make us ashamed," they kept telling Thomas.

But Thomas didn't care. "That was funny, that was

funny," he chuckled. He felt very pleased with himself.

Annie and Clarabel were deeply shocked. They had a great respect for Gordon the Big Engine.

Thomas left the coaches at a station and went to a mine for some freight cars.

Long ago, miners digging for lead had made tunnels under the ground.

Though strong enough to hold up freight cars, their roofs could not bear the weight of engines.

A large notice said: DANGER. ENGINES MUST NOT PASS THIS BOARD.

Thomas had often been warned, but he didn't care.

"Silly old board," he thought. He had often tried to pass it, but had never succeeded. This morning he laughed as he puffed

DANGER
ENGINES MUST
NOT PASS THIS
BOARD

along. He had made a plan.

He had to push empty freight cars into one siding and pull out full ones from another.

His Driver stopped him, and the Fireman went to turn the switches.

"Come on," waved the Fireman, and they started.

The Driver leaned out of the cab to see where they were going.

"Now!" said Thomas to himself and, bumping the freight cars fiercely, he jerked his Driver off the footplate.

"Hurrah!" laughed Thomas, and he followed the freight cars into the siding.

"Stupid old board!" said Thomas as he passed it. "There's no danger, there's no danger."

His Driver, unhurt, jumped up. "Look out!" he shouted.

The Fireman clambered into the cab. Thomas squealed crossly as his brakes were applied.

"It's quite safe," he hissed.

"Come back," yelled the Driver, but before they could move, there was rumbling and the rails quivered.

The Fireman jumped clear. As he did so, the ballast slipped away and the rails sagged and broke.

"Fire and smoke!" said Thomas. "I'm

sunk!" And he was!

Thomas could just see out of the hole, but he couldn't move.

"Oh, dear!" he said. "I am a silly engine."

"And a very naughty one, too," said a voice behind him. "I saw you."

"Please get me out; I won't be naughty again."

"I'm not so sure," replied Sir Topham Hatt. "We can't lift you out with a crane; the ground's not firm enough. Hmm . . . let me see . . . I wonder if Gordon could pull you out."

"Yes, Sir," said Thomas nervously. He didn't want to meet Gordon just yet!

"Down a mine, is he? Ho! Ho! Ho!" laughed Gordon.

"What a joke! What a joke!" he chortled, puffing to the rescue.

"*Poop! Poop!* Little Thomas," he whistled, "we'll have you out in a couple of puffs."

Strong cables were fastened between the two engines.

"*Poop! Poop! Poop!*"

"Are you ready? HEAVE," called Sir Topham Hatt.

But they didn't pull Thomas out in two puffs; Gordon was panting hard and nearly purple before he had dragged Thomas out of the hole and safely past the board.

"I'm sorry I was cheeky," said Thomas.

"That's all right, Thomas. You made me laugh. I like that. I'm in disgrace," Gordon went on pathetically.

"I feel very low."

"I'm in disgrace, too," said Thomas.

"Why, so you are, Thomas; we're both in disgrace. Shall we form an alliance?"

"An ally—what—was—it?"

"An alliance, Thomas. 'United we stand, together we fall,' " said Gordon grandly. "You help me, and I help you. How about it?"

"Right you are," said Thomas.

"Good! That's settled," rumbled Gordon.

And buffer to buffer the allies puffed home.

The stations on the line were being painted. The engines were surprised.

"The Queen is coming," said the painters. The engines in their Shed were excited and wondered who would pull the Royal Train.

"I'm too old to pull important trains," said Edward sadly.

"I'm in disgrace," Gordon said gloomily. "Sir

285

Topham Hatt would never choose me."

"He'll choose me, of course," boasted James the Red Engine.

"You!" Henry snorted. "*You* can't climb hills. He will ask *me* to pull it, *and* I'll have a new coat of paint. You wait and see."

The days passed. Henry puffed about proudly, quite sure that he would be the Royal Engine.

One day when it rained, his Driver and Fireman stretched a tarpaulin from the cab to the tender to keep themselves dry.

Henry puffed into the Big Station.

Paint Pots and Queens

A painter was climbing a ladder above the line. Henry's smoke puffed upward; it was thick and black. The painter choked and couldn't see. He missed his footing on the ladder, dropped his paint pot, and fell *plop* onto Henry's tarpaulin.

The paint poured over Henry's boiler and trickled down each side. The paint pot perched on his dome.

The painter clambered down and shook his brush at Henry.

"You spoil my clean paint with your dirty smoke," he said, "and then you take the whole lot and make me go and fetch some more." He stumped crossly away.

Sir Topham Hatt pushed through the crowd.

"You look like an iced cake, Henry," he said. "*That* won't do for the Royal Train. I must make other arrangements."

He walked over to the Yard.

Gordon and Thomas saw him coming, and both began to speak.

"Please, Sir—"

"One at a time," smiled Sir Topham Hatt. "Yes, Gordon?"

"May Thomas have his Branch Line again?"

"Hmm," said Sir Topham Hatt. "Well, Thomas?"

"Please, Sir, can Gordon pull coaches now?"

Sir Topham Hatt pondered.

"Hmm—you've both been quite good lately, and

you deserve a treat. When the Queen comes, Edward
will go in front and clear the line, Thomas will look
after the coaches, and Gordon—will pull the train."

"Ooooh, Sir!" said the engines happily.

The great day came. Percy, Toby, Henry, and James
worked hard bringing people to the town.

Thomas sorted all their coaches in the Yard.

"*Peep! Peep! Peep!* They're coming!" Edward
steamed in, looking smart with flags and bright paint.

Two minutes passed—five—seven—ten. *"Poop!
Poop!"* Everyone knew that whistle, and a mighty cheer
went up as the Queen's train glided into the station.

Gordon was spotless, and his brass shined. Like
Edward, he was decorated with flags, but on his buffer

beam he proudly carried the Royal Arms.

The Queen was met by Sir Topham Hatt, and before doing anything else, she thanked him for their splendid run.

"Not at all, Your Majesty," he said. "Thank *you*."

"We have read," said the Queen to Sir Topham Hatt, "a great deal about your engines. May we see them, please?"

So he led the way to where all the engines were waiting.

"*Peep! Peep!*" whistled Toby and Percy. "They're coming!"

"Shh, shh! Shh, shh!" hissed Henry and James.

But Toby and Percy were too excited to care.

Sir Topham Hatt told the Queen their names, and she talked to each engine. Then she turned to go.

Percy bubbled over. "Three cheers for the Queen!" he called.

"*Peeeep! Peeeep! Peeeep!*" whistled all the engines.

Sir Topham Hatt held his ears, but the Queen,

smiling, waved to the engines till she passed the gate.

The next day, the Queen spoke specially to Thomas, who fetched her coaches, and to Edward and Gordon, who took her away; and no engines ever felt prouder than Thomas, Edward, and Gordon the Big Engine.

THE RAILWAY SERIES

SINCE 1945

Edward the Blue Engine

 Cows!

 Bertie's Chase

 Saved from Scrap

 Old Iron

Edward the Blue Engine

THE REV. W. AWDRY

with illustrations by

C. REGINALD DALBY

DEAR FRIENDS,

I think most of you are fond of Edward. His Driver and Fireman, Charlie Sand and Sidney Hever, are fond of him, too. They were very pleased when they knew I was giving Edward a book all to himself.

Edward is old, and some of the other engines were rude about the clanking noise he made as he did his work.

They aren't rude now! These stories tell you why.

THE AUTHOR

Cows!

Edward the Blue Engine was getting old. His bearings were worn, and he clanked as he puffed along. He was taking twenty empty cattle cars to a market town.

The sun shined, the birds sang, and some cows grazed in a field by the line.

"Come on! Come on! Come on!" puffed Edward.

"Oh! Oh! Oh! Oh!" screamed the cattle cars.

Edward puffed and clanked; the cattle cars rattled and screamed. The cows were not used to trains. The noise and smoke disturbed them.

They twitched up their tails and ran.

They galloped across the field, broke through the fence, and charged the train between the thirteenth and fourteenth cattle cars. The coupling broke, and the last seven cattle cars left the rails. They were not damaged and stayed upright. They ran for a short way along the sleepers before stopping.

Edward felt a jerk but didn't take much notice.
He was used to all kinds of freight cars.

"Bother those cattle cars!" he thought. "Why can't
they come quietly?" He ran on to the next station
before either he or his Driver realized what had
happened.

When Gordon and Henry heard about the
accident, they laughed and laughed. "Fancy allowing
cows to break his train! They wouldn't dare do that
to us. We'd show them!" they boasted.

Edward pretended not to mind, but Toby was cross.

"You couldn't help it, Edward," he said. "They've never met cows. I have, and I know the trouble they are."

Some days later, Gordon rushed through Edward's station.

"*Poop, poop!*" he whistled. "Mind the cows!"

"Haha, haha, haha!" he chortled, panting up the hill.

"Hurry, hurry, hurry!" puffed Gordon.

"Don't make such a fuss! Don't make such a fuss!" grumbled his coaches. They rumbled over the viaduct and roared through the next station.

A long straight stretch of line lay ahead. In the distance was a bridge. It had high parapets on each side.

It seemed to Gordon that there was something on the bridge. His Driver thought so, too. "Whoa, Gordon!" he said, and shut off steam.

"*Pooh!*" said Gordon. "It's only a cow!

"Shoo! Shoo!" he hissed, moving slowly onto the bridge.

But the cow wouldn't shoo! She had lost her calf and felt lonely. "Moooo!" she said sadly, walking towards him.

Gordon stopped!

His Driver, Fireman, and some passengers tried to send her away, but she wouldn't go, so they gave it up.

Presently, Henry arrived with a train from the other direction.

"What's this?" he said grandly. "A cow? I'll soon settle her. Be off! Be off!" he puffed. But the cow turned and mooed at him. Henry backed away. "I don't want to hurt her," he said.

Drivers, Firemen, and passengers again tried to move the cow, but failed. Henry's Guard went back and put flares on the line to protect his train. At the nearest station, he told them about the cow.

"That must be Bluebell," said a porter thoughtfully. "Her calf is here, ready to go to market. We'll take it along."

So they unloaded the calf and took it to the bridge.

"Moo! Moo!" wailed the calf. "Moo! Moo!" bellowed Bluebell.

She nuzzled her calf happily, and the porter led them away.

The two trains started.

"Not a word."

"Keep it dark," whispered Gordon and Henry as they passed, but the story soon spread.

"Well, well, well!" chuckled Edward. "Two big engines afraid of one cow!"

"Afraid——Rubbish," said Gordon huffily. "We didn't want the poor thing to hurt herself by running against us. We stopped so as not to excite her. You see what I mean, my dear Edward."

"Yes, Gordon," said Edward gravely.

Gordon felt somehow that Edward "saw" only too well.

Bertie's Chase

"*Peep! Peep!* We're late," fussed Edward. "*Peep! Peeppipeep!* Where is Thomas? He doesn't usually make us wait."

"Oh, dear, what can the matter be? . . . ," sang the Fireman, "Johnnie's so long at . . ."

"Never you mind about Johnnie," laughed the Driver, "just you climb on the cab and look for Thomas.

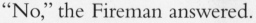

"Can you see him?"

"No," the Fireman answered.

The Guard looked at his watch. "Ten minutes late!" he said to the Driver. "We can't wait here all day."

"Look again, Sid," said the Driver, "just in case. Can you see him?"

"Not Thomas," answered the Fireman, "but there's Bertie the Bus in a tearing hurry. No need to bother with him, though. Likely he's on a Coach Tour or something." He clambered down.

"Right away, Charlie," said the Guard, and Edward puffed off.

"*Toooot! Toooot!* Stop! Stop!" wailed Bertie, roaring into the Yard, but it was no good. Edward's last coach had disappeared into the tunnel.

"Bother!" said Bertie. "Bother Thomas' Fireman not coming to work today. Oh, why did I promise to help the passengers catch the train?"

"That will do, Bertie," said his Driver. "A promise is a promise, and we must keep it."

"I'll catch Edward or bust," said Bertie grimly as he raced along the road.

"Oh, my gears and axles!" he groaned, toiling up the hill. "I'll never be the same bus again!"

"*Tootootoo! Tootoot!* I see him. Hurray! Hurray!" he cheered as he reached the top of the hill.

"He's reached the station," Bertie groaned the next minute.

"No . . . he's stopped by a signal. Hurray! Hurray!" And he tore down the hill, his brakes squealing at the corners.

His passengers bounced like balls in a bucket. "Well done, Bertie," they shouted. "Go! Go!"

Hens and dogs scattered in all directions as Bertie raced through the village.

"Wait! Wait!" he tooted, skidding into the Yard.

He was just in time to see the signal drop, the Guard wave his flag, and Edward puff out of the station.

His passengers rushed to the platform, but it was no good, and they came bustling back.

"I'm sorry," said Bertie unhappily.

"Never mind, Bertie," they said. "After him quickly. Third time lucky, you know!"

"Do you think we'll catch him at the next station, Driver?"

"There's a good chance," he answered. "Our road keeps close to the line, and we can climb hills better than Edward."

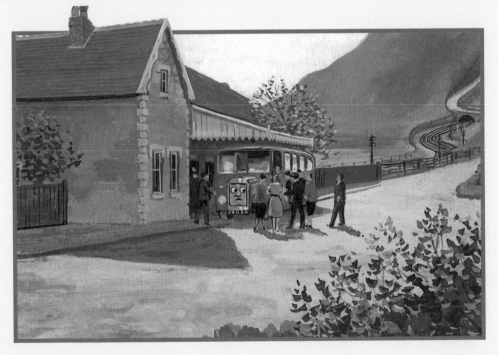

He thought for a minute. "I'll just make sure." He then spoke to the Station Master while the passengers waited impatiently in the bus.

"This hill is too steep! This hill is too steep!" grumbled the coaches as Edward snorted in front.

They reached the top at last and ran smoothly into the station.

"*Peepeep!*" whistled Edward. "Get in quickly, please."

The porters and people hurried, and Edward impatiently waited to start.

"*Peeeep!*" whistled the Guard, and Edward's Driver

looked back, but the flag didn't wave. There was a distant *"Tooootoooot!"* and the Station Master, running across, snatched the green flag out of the Guard's hand.

Then everything seemed to happen at once.

"Too-too-toooooot!" bellowed Bertie. His passengers poured onto the platform and scrambled into the train. The Station Master told the Guard and Driver what had happened, and Edward listened.

"I'm sorry about the chase, Bertie," he said.

"My fault," panted Bertie, "late at junction. . . . You didn't know . . . about Thomas' passengers."

"Peepeep! Goodbye, Bertie. We're off!" whistled Edward.

"Three cheers for Bertie!" called the passengers. They cheered and waved till they were out of sight.

Saved from Scrap

There is a scrap yard near Edward's station. It is full of rusty old cars and machinery. They are brought there to be broken up. The pieces are loaded into freight cars, and Edward pulls them to the Steelworks, where they are melted down and used again.

One day, Edward saw a traction engine in the scrap yard.

"Hullo!" he said. "You're not broken and rusty. What are *you* doing there?"

"I'm Trevor," said the traction engine sadly. "They are going to break me up next week."

"What a shame!" said Edward.

"My Driver says I only need some paint, Brasso, and oil to be as good as new," Trevor went on sadly. "But it's no good. My Master doesn't want me. I suppose it's because I'm old-fashioned."

Edward snorted indignantly. "People say *I'm* old-fashioned, but I don't care. Sir Topham Hatt says I'm a

Useful Engine."

"My Driver says I'm useful, too," replied Trevor. "I sometimes feel ill, but I don't give up like these tractors; I struggle on and finish the job. I've never broken down in my life," he ended proudly.

"What work did you do?" asked Edward kindly.

"My Master would send us from farm to farm. We threshed the corn, hauled logs, sawed timber, and did lots of other work. We made friends at all the farms and saw them every year. The children loved to see us come.

They followed us in crowds and watched us all day long. My Driver would sometimes give them rides."

Trevor shut his eyes—remembering—"I like children," he said simply. "Oh, yes, I like children."

"Broken up, what a shame! Broken up, what a shame!" clanked Edward as he went back to work. "I *must* help Trevor. I *must*!"

He thought of the people he knew who liked engines. Edward had lots of friends, but strangely none of them had room for a traction engine at home!

"It's a shame! It's a shame!" he hissed as he brought his coaches to the station.

Then——

"Peep! Peep!" he whistled. "Why didn't I think of him before?"

Waiting there on the platform was the very person. It was the Vicar.

"'Morning, Charlie. 'Morning, Sid. Hullo, Edward, you look upset!"

"What's the matter, Charlie?" he asked the Driver.

"There's a traction engine in the scrap yard, Vicar," the Driver said. "He'll be broken up next week, and it's a shame. Jem Cole says he never drove a better engine."

"Do save him, sir! You've got room, sir!" Edward said.

"Yes, Edward, I've got room," laughed the Vicar,

"but I don't need a traction engine!"

"He'll saw wood and give children rides. Do buy him, sir, please!"

"We'll see," said the Vicar, and climbed into the train.

Jem Cole came on Saturday afternoon. "The Reverend's coming to see you, Trevor. Maybe he'll buy you."

"Do you think he will?" asked Trevor hopefully.

"He will when I've lit your fire and cleaned you up," said Jem.

When the Vicar and his two boys arrived in the evening, Trevor was blowing off steam. He hadn't felt so happy for months.

"Watch this, Reverend," called Jem, and Trevor chuffered happily about the yard.

"Oh, Daddy, do buy him," pleaded the boys, jumping up and down in their excitement.

"Now *I'll* try," said the Vicar, climbing up beside Jem.

"Show your paces, Trevor," he said, and drove him about the yard.

Then he went into the office and came out smiling. "I've got him cheap, Jem, cheap."

"D'ye hear that, Trevor?" cried Jem. "The Reverend's saved you, and you'll live at the Vicarage now."

"Peep! Peep!" whistled Trevor happily.

"Will you drive him home for me, Jem, and take these scallywags with you? They won't want to come in the car when there's a traction engine to ride on!"

Trevor's home in the Vicarage Orchard is close to the railway, and he sees Edward every day. His paint is spotless and his brass shines like gold.

He saws firewood in winter, and Jem sometimes borrows him when a tractor fails. Trevor likes doing his old jobs, but his happiest day is the Church Fête. Then, with a long wooden seat bolted to his bunker, he chuffers round the Orchard, giving rides to children.

Long afterwards, you will see him shut his eyes— remembering—"I like children," he whispers happily.

Old Iron

One day, James had to wait at Edward's station till Edward and his train came in. This made him cross. "Late again!" he shouted.

Edward only laughed, and James fumed away.

"Edward is impossible," he grumbled to the others. "He clanks about like a lot of old iron, and he is so slow he makes us wait."

Thomas and Percy were indignant. "Old iron!" they snorted. "Slow! Why, Edward could beat you in a race any day!"

"Really!" said James huffily. "I should like to see him do it."

One day, James' Driver did not feel well when he came to work. "I'll manage," he said. But when they reached the top of Gordon's Hill, he could hardly stand.

The Fireman drove the train to the next station. He spoke to the Signalman, put the coaches in a siding, and uncoupled James ready for shunting.

Then he helped the Driver over to the station and asked them to look after him and find a "Relief."

Suddenly, the Signalman shouted, and the Fireman turned round and saw James puffing away.

He ran hard, but he couldn't catch James and soon came back to the signal box. The Signalman was busy. "All traffic halted," he announced at last. "Up and down, main lines are clear for thirty miles, and the Inspector's coming."

The Fireman mopped his face. "What happened?" he asked.

"Two boys were on the footplate. They tumbled off when James started. I shouted at them, and they ran like rabbits."

"Just let me catch them," said the Fireman grimly.

"I'll teach them to meddle with my engine."

Both men jumped as the telephone rang. "Yes," answered the Signalman, "he's here. . . . Right, I'll tell him.

"The Inspector's coming at once in Edward. He wants a shunter's pole and a coil of wire rope."

"What for?" wondered the Fireman.

"Search me! But you'd better get them quickly."

The Fireman was ready and waiting when Edward arrived. The Inspector saw the pole and rope. "Good man," he said. "Jump in."

"We'll catch him, we'll catch him," puffed Edward, crossing to the up line in pursuit.

James was laughing as he left the Yard. "What a lark! What a lark!" he chuckled to himself.

Presently, he missed his Driver's hand on the regulator... and then he realized there was no one in his cab....

"What shall I do?" he wailed. "I can't stop. Help! Help!"

"We're coming, we're coming."

Edward was panting up behind with every ounce

of steam he had. With a great effort, he caught up and crept alongside, slowly gaining till his smokebox was level with James' buffer beam.

"Steady, Edward."

The Inspector stood on Edward's front, holding a noose of rope in the crook of the shunter's pole. He was trying to slip it over James' buffer. The engines swayed and lurched. He tried again and again. More than once, he nearly fell but just saved himself.

At last—— "Got him!" he shouted. He pulled the

noose tight and came back to the cab safely.

Gently braking so as not to snap the rope, Edward's Driver checked the engines' speed, and James' Fireman scrambled across and took control.

The engines puffed back side by side. "So the 'old iron' caught you after all!" chuckled Edward.

"I'm sorry," whispered James. "Thank you for saving me."

"That's all right."

"You were splendid, Edward."

Sir Topham Hatt was waiting and thanking the men warmly. "A fine piece of work," he said. "James, you can rest and then take your train. I'm proud of you, Edward. You shall go to the Works and have your worn parts mended."

"Oh! Thank you, Sir!" said Edward happily. "It'll be *lovely* not to clank."

The two naughty boys were soon caught by the police, and their fathers walloped them soundly.

They were also forbidden to watch trains till they could be trusted.

James' Driver soon got well in hospital and is now back at work.

James missed him very much, but he missed Edward more. And you will be glad to know that when Edward came home the other day, James and all the other engines gave him a tremendous welcome.

Sir Topham Hatt thinks he will be deaf for weeks!

Four Little Engines

 Skarloey Remembers

 Sir Handel

 Peter Sam and the
Refreshment Lady

 Old Faithful

Four Little Engines

THE REV. W. AWDRY

with illustrations by

C. REGINALD DALBY

DEAR FRIENDS,

Sir Handel Brown is the owner of a little railway which goes to Skarloey and Rheneas. Skarloey means "Lake in the Woods," and Rheneas means "Divided Waterfall." They are beautiful places, and lots of people visit them.

The Owner is very busy, so Mr. Peter Sam manages the railway.

The two engines, who are called Skarloey and Rheneas, grew old and tired, so the Owner bought two others.

The stories tell you what happened.

THE AUTHOR

Skarloey Remembers

S ir Topham Hatt had sent Edward to the Works to
be mended. Near the Works Station, Edward
noticed a narrow-gauge engine standing in an
open-sided shed.

"That's Skarloey," he thought. "What's he doing
there?" He remembered Skarloey and his brother,
Rheneas, because in the old days he had often

brought passengers who wanted to travel up to the Lake in their little train.

As the men at the Works could not mend him at once, Edward asked them to put him on a siding close to Skarloey.

Skarloey was pleased to see Edward.

"The Owner, Sir Handel Brown, has just bought two more engines," he said.

"He told me I was a Very Old Engine and deserved a good rest. He gave me this shed so that I could see everything and not be lonely. But I am lonely all the same," he continued sadly. "I miss Rheneas very

much. Yesterday one of the new engines pushed him on a flatbed, and now he's gone to be mended.

"I wish I could be mended, too, and pull coaches again."

"Have your coaches got names?" asked Edward.

"Oh, yes, there's Agnes, Ruth, Jemima, Lucy, and Beatrice. Agnes is proud. She has cushions for first-class passengers. She pities Ruth, Jemima, and Lucy, who are third-class with bare boards; but they, all four, sniff at Beatrice. Beatrice often smells of fish and cheese, but she is *most* important," said Skarloey earnestly. "She has a little window through which the Guard sells tickets.

I sometimes leave the others behind, but I always take Beatrice. You *must* have tickets and a Guard, you know."

"Of course," said Edward gravely.

"Rheneas and I," continued Skarloey, "used to take turns at pulling the trains. We know everybody, and everybody knows us. We whistle to the people in the fields, at level crossings, and in lonely cottages and farms, and the people always wave to us.

"We love passing the school playgrounds at break-time, for then the children will always run over to the fence to watch us go by. The passengers always wave because they think the children are waving to them; but we engines know better, of course," said Skarloey importantly.

"Yes, we do indeed," agreed Edward.

"We take your tourists to the Lake and then get ready to pull the train back.

"We enjoy the morning journey home because then our friends from the villages come down to do their shopping.

"We whistle before every station, *'Peep! Peeeep! Look out!'* and the people are there ready.

" 'Where's Mrs. Last?' asks the Guard.

" 'She's coming.'

" *'Peep peeeeeep!'* we whistle, and Mrs. Last comes

running onto the platform. 'We'll leave you behind one of these days, Missis,' laughs our Driver, but we know he never will.

"We stop elsewhere, too, at farm crossings and stiles, where paths lead to lonely houses. Rheneas and I know all the places very well indeed. Our Driver used to say that we would stop even if he didn't put on the brakes!

"Sometimes, on market day, Ruth, Jemima, and Lucy were so full of people that the Guard would allow third-class passengers to travel in Agnes. She

didn't like that at all and would rumble. 'First——class——coach——third——class——people.'

"That made me cross. 'Hush!' I'd say, 'or I'll bump you!' That soon stopped her rudeness to my friends."

Just then some workmen came. "We're going to mend you now, Edward," they said. "Come along."

"Goodbye, Skarloey. Thank you for telling me about your railway. It's a lovely little line."

"It is! It is! Thank you for talking to me, Edward. You've cheered me up. Goodbye!"

Skarloey watched Edward being taken back to the

Works. Then, shutting his eyes, he dozed in the warm afternoon sun. He smiled as he dozed, for he was dreaming, as old engines will, of happy days in the past.

Sir Handel

The new engines looked very smart. One was
called Sir Handel and the other Peter Sam.

"What a small shed!" grumbled Sir Handel. "This
won't do at all!"

"I think it's nice," said Peter Sam.

"Huh!" grunted Sir Handel. "What's that rubbish?"

"Shh, shh!" said Peter Sam, "that's Skarloey, the famous old engine.

"I'm sorry, Skarloey." He whispered, "Sir Handel's upset now, but he's quite nice really."

Skarloey felt sorry for Peter Sam.

"Now, Sir Handel," said the Fireman next morning, "we'll get you ready."

"I'm tired," he yawned. "Let Peter Sam go. He'd love it."

"No," said the Fireman. "Owner's orders, you're first."

"Oh, well!" said Sir Handel sulkily. "I suppose I must."

When his Driver arrived, Sir Handel puffed away to fetch the coaches.

"Whatever next?" he snorted. "Those aren't coaches, they're cattle cars!"

"Ooooooh!" screamed Agnes, Ruth, Lucy, Jemima, and Beatrice. "What a horrid engine!"

"It's not what I'm used to," clanked Sir Handel rebelliously, making for the station.

He rolled to the platform just as Gordon arrived.

"Hullo!" he said. "Who are you?"

"I'm Gordon. Who are you?"

"I'm Sir Handel. Yes, I've heard of you; you're an Express engine, I believe. So am I, but I'm used to fancy coaches, not these cattle cars. Do you have fancy coaches? Oh, yes, I see you do. We must have a chat sometime. Sorry I can't stop; must keep time, you know."

And he puffed off, leaving Gordon at a loss for words!

"Come along! COME ALONG!" Sir Handel puffed.

"Cattle cars! CATTLE CARS!" grumbled the coaches. "We'll pay him back! WE'LL PAY HIM BACK!"

Presently they stopped at a station. The line curved here and began to climb. It was not very steep, but the day was misty and the rails were slippery.

"Hold back!" whispered Agnes to Ruth. "Hold back!" whispered Ruth to Jemima. "Hold back!" whispered Jemima to Lucy. "Hold back!" whispered Lucy to Beatrice, and they giggled as Sir Handel started and their couplings tightened.

"Come on! COME ON!" he puffed as his wheels slipped on the greasy rails. "Come on, come on, COME ON, COME ON!"

His wheels were spinning, but the coaches pulled

him back, and the train stopped on the hill beyond the station. "I can't do it, I can't do it," he grumbled. "I'm used to sensible fancy coaches, not these bumpy cattle cars." The Guard came up. "I think the coaches are up to something," he told the Driver. So they decided to bring the train down again to a level piece of line to give Sir Handel a good start.

The Guard helped the Fireman put sand on the rails, and Sir Handel made a tremendous effort. The coaches tried hard to drag him back, but he puffed and pulled so hard that they were soon over the top and away on their journey.

The Line Manager, Mr. Peter Sam, was severe with

Sir Handel that night.

"You are a Troublesome Engine," he said. "You are rude, conceited, and much too big for your wheels. Next time I shall punish you severely."

Sir Handel was impressed and behaved well for several days!

Then, one morning, he took the train to the Top Station. He was cross; it was Peter Sam's turn, but the Line Manager had made him go instead.

"We'll leave the coaches," said his Driver, "and fetch

some freight cars from the Quarry."

"Freight cars!" snorted Sir Handel, "FREIGHT CARS!"

"Yes," his Driver repeated, "freight cars."

Sir Handel jerked forward. "I won't!" he muttered. "So there!" He lurched, bumped, and stopped. His Driver and Fireman got out.

"Told you!" said Sir Handel triumphantly.

He had pushed the rails apart and settled down between them.

They telephoned the Line Manager. He came up at once with Peter Sam and brought some workmen in a coach. Then he and the Fireman took Peter Sam home with Sir Handel's coaches, while the Driver and the workmen put Sir Handel back on the rails.

Sir Handel did not feel so pleased with himself when he crawled home and found the Line Manager waiting for him. "You are a very naughty engine," he said sternly. "You will stay in the shed till I can trust you to behave."

Peter Sam and the Refreshment Lady

As Sir Handel was shut up, Peter Sam had to run the line. He was excited, and the Fireman found it hard to get him ready.

"Sober up, can't you!" he growled.

"Anybody would think," said Sir Handel rudely, "that he *wanted* to work."

"All *respectable* engines do," said Skarloey firmly. "I wish I could work myself. Keep calm, Peter Sam. Don't get excited, and you'll do very well."

But Peter Sam was in such a state that he couldn't listen.

When his Driver came, Peter Sam ran along to fetch the coaches. "*Peep, pip, pip, peep!* Come along, girls!" he whistled, and although he was so excited, he remembered to be careful. "That's the way, my dears, gently does it."

"What did he say?" asked Jemima, who was deaf.

"He said, 'Come along, girls,' and he . . . he called us his 'dears,' " simpered the other coaches. "Really one does not know *what* to think . . . such a handsome young engine, too . . . *so* nice and well mannered." And they tittered happily together as they followed Peter Sam.

Peter Sam fussed into the station to find Henry already there.

"This won't do, youngster," said Henry. "*I* can't be kept waiting. If you are late tonight, I'll go off and leave your passengers behind."

"Pooh!" said Peter Sam, but secretly he was a little worried.

But he couldn't feel worried for long.

"What fun it all is," he thought as he ran round his train.

He let off steam happily while he waited for the Guard to blow his whistle and wave his green flag.

Peter Sam puffed happily away, singing a little song. "I'm Peter Sam! I'm running this line! I'm Peter Sam! I'm running this line!"

The people waved as he passed the farms and cottages, and he gave a loud whistle at the school.

The children all ran to see him puffing by.

Agnes, Ruth, Jemima, Lucy, and Beatrice enjoyed themselves, too. "He's cocky . . . *trock, trock* . . . but he's nice . . . *trock, trock;* he's cocky . . . *trock, trock . . .*

but he's nice... *trock, trock,*" they sang as they
trundled along. They were growing very fond of
Peter Sam.

Every afternoon, they had to wait an hour at the
station by the Lake.

The Driver, the Fireman, and the Guard usually
bought something from the Refreshment Lady and
went and sat in Beatrice. The Refreshment Lady
always came home on this train.

Time passed slowly today for Peter Sam.

At last, his Driver and Fireman came. "*Peep, peeeeeep!* Hurry up, please!*" he whistled to the passengers, and they came strolling back to the station.

Peter Sam was sizzling with impatience. "How awful," he thought, "if we miss Henry's train."

The last passengers arrived. The Guard was ready with his flag and whistle. The Refreshment Lady walked across the platform.

Then it happened!

The Guard says that Peter Sam was too impatient; Peter Sam says he was sure he heard a whistle.... Anyway, he started.

"Come quickly, come quickly!" he puffed.

"Stop! . . . Stop! . . . STOP!" wailed the coaches. "You've . . . left . . . her . . . behind . . . ! YOU'VE . . . LEFT . . . HER . . . BEHIND . . . !"

The Guard whistled and waved his red flag. The Driver, looking back, saw the Refreshment Lady shouting and running after the train.

"Bother!" groaned Peter Sam as he stopped. "We'll miss Henry now." The Refreshment Lady climbed into Beatrice, and they started again. "We're sure to be late! We're sure to be late!" panted Peter Sam frantically. His Driver had to keep checking him. "Steady, old boy, steady."

"*Peep, peep!*" Peter Sam whistled at the stations. "Hurry! Please hurry!" And they reached the Big Station just as Henry steamed in.

"Hurrah!" said Peter Sam. "We've caught him after all." And he let off steam with relief. "*Whooooosh!*"

"Not bad, youngster," said Henry loftily.

The Refreshment Lady shook her fist at Peter Sam. "What do you mean by leaving me behind?" she demanded.

"I'm sorry, Refreshment Lady, but I was worried about our passengers." And he told her what Henry had said.

The Refreshment Lady laughed. "You silly engine!" she said. "Henry wouldn't dare go; he's *got* to wait. It's a *guaranteed connection*!"

"Well!" said Peter Sam. "Well! Where's that Henry?"

But Peter Sam was too late that time, for Henry had chortled away!

Old Faithful

Sir Handel stayed shut up for several days. But one market day, Peter Sam could not work; he needed repairs.

Sir Handel was glad to come out. He tried to be kind, but the coaches didn't trust him. They were awkward and rude. He even sang them little songs, but it was no use.

It was most unfortunate, too, that Sir Handel had to check suddenly to avoid running over a sheep.

"He's bumped us!" screamed the coaches. "Let's pay him back!"

The coaches knew that all engines must go carefully at a place near the Big Station. But they were so cross with Sir Handel that they didn't care what they did. They surged into Sir Handel, making him lurch off the line. Luckily no one was hurt.

Sir Handel limped to the shed. Mr. Peter Sam, the

Line Manager, inspected the damage. "No more work for you today," he said. "Bother those coaches! We must take the village people home and fetch the tourists, all without an engine."

"What about me, sir?" said a voice.

"Skarloey!" he exclaimed. "Can you do it?"

"I'll try," answered the old engine.

The coaches stood at the platform. Skarloey advanced on them, hissing crossly. "I'm ashamed of you," he scolded. "Such behavior—you might have hurt your passengers. On market day, too!"

"We're sorry, Skarloey, we didn't think; it's that Sir Handel, he's . . ."

"No tales," said Skarloey firmly. "I won't have it, and

don't you dare try tricks on me."

"No, Skarloey, of course not, Skarloey," quavered the coaches meekly.

Skarloey might be old and have dirty paint, but he was certainly an engine who would stand no nonsense.

His friends crowded round, and the Guard had to shoo them away before they could start. Skarloey felt happy; he remembered all the gates and stiles where he had to stop and whistled to his friends. The sun shined and the rails were dry. "This is lovely," he thought.

But presently, they began to climb and he felt short of steam.

"Bother my tubes!" he panted.

"Take your time, old boy," soothed his Driver.

"I'll manage, I'll manage," he wheezed, and, pausing for "breath" at the stations, he gallantly struggled along.

After a rest at the Top Station, Skarloey was ready to start.

"It'll be better downhill," he thought.

The coaches ran nicely, but he soon began to feel tired again. His springs were weak, and the rail-joints jarred his wheels.

Then, with a crack, a front spring broke, and he stopped.

"I feel all crooked," he complained.

"That's torn it," said his Driver. "We'll need a bus now for our passengers."

"No!" pleaded Skarloey. "I'd be ashamed to have a bus take my passengers. I'll get home or bust," he promised bravely.

The Line Manager looked at his watch and paced the platform. James and his train waited impatiently, too.

They heard a hoarse *"Peep! Peep!"* then, groaning, clanging, and clanking, Skarloey crept into sight. He was tilted to one side and making fearful noises, but he plodded bravely on.

"I'll *do* it, I'll *do* it," he gasped between the clanks

364

and groans, "I'll... I've done it!" And he sighed thankfully as the train stopped where James was waiting.

James said nothing. He waited for his passengers and then respectfully puffed away.

"You were right, Sir," said Skarloey to the Owner that evening, "old engines can't pull trains like young ones."

The Owner smiled. "They can if they're mended, Old Faithful," he said, "and that's what will happen to you. You deserve it."

"Oh, Sir!" said Skarloey happily. Sir Handel is longing for Skarloey to come back.

He thinks Skarloey is the best engine in the world. He does his fair share of the work now, and the coaches never play tricks on him because he always manages them in "Skarloey's way."

If you have enjoyed these stories, you will enjoy a visit to the Talyllyn Railway at Towyn in Wales.

Percy the Small Engine

Percy the Small Engine

THE REV. W. AWDRY
with illustrations by
C. REGINALD DALBY

DEAR CHRISTOPHER, AND GILES, AND PETER,
AND CLIVE,

Thank you for writing to ask for a book about
Percy. He is still cheeky, and we were afraid (Sir
Topham Hatt and I) that if he had a book to
himself, it might make him cheekier than ever, and
that would never do!

But Percy has been such a Really Useful Engine
that we both think he deserves a book. Here it is.

THE AUTHOR

Percy and the Signal

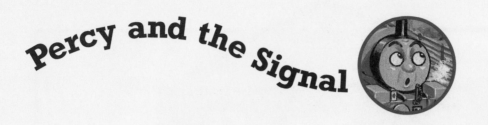

Percy is a little green tank engine who works in the Yard at the Big Station. He is a funny little engine and loves playing jokes. These jokes sometimes get him into trouble.

"*Peep, peep!*" he whistled one morning. "Hurry up, Gordon! The train's ready."

Gordon thought he was late and came puffing out.

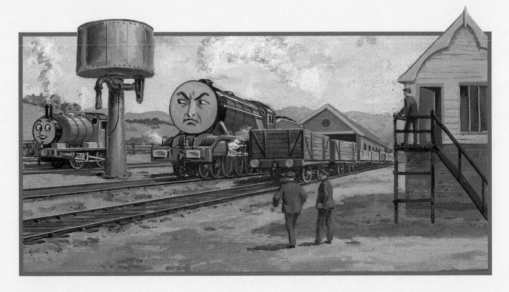

"Ha ha!" laughed Percy, and showed him a train of dirty coal cars.

Gordon didn't go back to the Shed.

He stayed on a siding, thinking how to get Percy back.

"Stay in the Shed today," squeaked Percy to James. "Sir Topham Hatt will come and see you."

James was a conceited engine. "Ah!" he thought. "Sir Topham Hatt knows I'm a fine engine, ready for anything. He wants me to pull a Special Train."

So James stayed where he was, and nothing his Driver and Fireman could do would make him move.

But Sir Topham Hatt never came, and the other

engines grumbled dreadfully.

They had to do James' work as well as their own.

At last an Inspector came. "Shake a wheel, James," he said crossly. "You can't stay here all day."

"Sir Topham Hatt told me to stay here," answered James sulkily. "He sent a message this morning."

"He did not," retorted the Inspector. "How could he? He's away for a week."

"Oh!" said James. "Oh!" And he came quickly out of the Shed. "Where's Percy?" Percy had wisely disappeared!

When Sir Topham Hatt came back, he *did* see James, and Percy, too. Both engines wished he hadn't!

James and Gordon wanted to get Percy back, but Percy kept out of their way. One morning, however, he was so excited that he forgot to be careful.

"I say, you engines," he bubbled, "I'm taking some freight cars to Thomas' Junction. Sir Topham Hatt chose me specially. He must know I'm a Really Useful Engine."

"More likely he wants you out of the way," grunted James.

But Gordon gave James a wink. . . . Like this.

"Ah, yes," said James, "just so. . . . You were saying,

Gordon...?"

"James and I were just speaking about signals at the
junction. We can't be too careful about signals. But
then, I needn't say that to a Really Useful Engine like
you, Percy."

Percy felt flattered.

"Of course not," he said.

"We had spoken of 'backing signals,' " put in James.
"They need extra special care, you know. Would you
like me to explain?"

"No, thank you, James," said Percy airily. "I know all

about signals." And he bustled off importantly.

James and Gordon solemnly exchanged winks!

Percy was a little worried as he set out.

"I wonder what 'backing signals' are?" he thought. "Never mind, I'll manage. I know all about signals." He puffed crossly to his freight cars and felt better.

He saw a signal just outside the station. "Bother!" he said. "It's at 'danger.' "

"Oh! Oh! Oh!" screamed the freight cars as they bumped into each other.

Presently, the signal moved to show "line clear." Its arm moved up instead of down. Percy had never seen that sort of signal before. He was surprised.

" 'Down' means 'go,' " he thought, "and 'up' means 'stop,' so 'upper still' must mean 'go back.' I know! It's one of those 'backing signals.' How clever of me to find that out."

"Come on, Percy," said his Driver, "off we go."

But Percy wouldn't go forward, and his Driver had to let him "back" in order to start at all.

"I am clever," thought Percy. "Even my Driver

doesn't know about 'backing signals.'" And he started so suddenly that the freight cars screamed again.

"Whoa! Percy," called his Driver. "Stop! You're going the wrong way."

"But it's a 'backing signal,'" Percy protested, and told him about Gordon and James. The Driver laughed and explained about signals that point up.

"Oh, dear!" said Percy. "Let's start quickly before they come and see us."

But he was too late. Gordon swept by with the Express and saw everything.

The big engines talked about signals that night. They thought the subject was funny. They laughed a lot. Percy thought they were being very silly!

Duck Takes Charge

"Do you know what?" asked Percy.

"What?" grunted Gordon.

"Do you know what?"

"Silly," said Gordon crossly, "of course I don't know what, if you don't tell me what what is."

"Sir Topham Hatt says that the work in the Yard is too heavy for me. He's getting a bigger engine to help me."

"Rubbish!" put in James. "Any engine could do it," he went on grandly. "If you worked more and chattered less, this Yard would be a sweeter, a better, and a happier place."

Percy went off to fetch some coaches.

"That stupid old signal," he thought. "No one listens to me now. They think I'm a silly little engine and order me about.

"I'll show them! I'll show them!" he puffed as he ran about the Yard. But he didn't know how.

Things went wrong, the coaches and freight cars behaved badly, and by the end of the afternoon he felt tired and unhappy.

He brought some coaches to the station and stood panting at the end of the platform.

"Hullo, Percy!" said Sir Topham Hatt. "You look tired."

"Yes, Sir. I am, Sir; I don't know if I'm standing on my dome or my wheels."

"You look the right way up to me," laughed Sir Topham Hatt. "Cheer up! The new engine is bigger than you and can probably do the work alone. Would you like to help build my new harbor at Thomas' Junction? Thomas and Toby will help, but I need an engine there all the time."

"Oh, yes, Sir. Thank you, Sir!" said Percy happily.

The new engine arrived the next morning.

"What is your name?" asked Sir Topham Hatt kindly.

"Montague, Sir; but I'm usually called 'Duck.' They say I waddle; I don't really, Sir, but I like 'Duck' better than Montague."

"Good!" said Sir Topham Hatt. " 'Duck' it shall be. Here, Percy, come and show Duck round."

The two engines went off together. At first the freight cars played tricks, but soon found that playing tricks on Duck was a mistake! The coaches behaved well, though James, Gordon, and Henry did not.

382

They watched Duck quietly doing his work. "He seems a simple sort of engine," they whispered. "We'll have some fun.

"Quaa-aa-aak! Quaa-aa-aak!" they wheezed as they passed him.

Percy was cross, but Duck took no notice. "They'll get tired of it soon," he said.

Presently the three engines began to order Duck about.

Duck stopped. "Do they tell you to do things, Percy?" he asked.

"Yes, they do," answered Percy sadly.

"Right," said Duck, "we'll soon stop *that* nonsense." He whispered something. . . . "We'll do it tonight."

Sir Topham Hatt had had a good day. There had been no grumbling passengers, all the trains had run on time, and Duck had worked well in the Yard.

Sir Topham Hatt was looking forward to hot buttered toast for tea at home.

He had just left the office when he heard an extraordinary noise.

"Bother!" he said, and hurried to the Yard.

Henry, Gordon, and James were *wheeeeeshi*ng and snorting furiously, while Duck and Percy calmly sat on the switches outside the Shed, refusing to let the engines in.

"STOP THAT NOISE," he bellowed.

"Now, Gordon."

"They won't let us in," hissed the big engine crossly.

"Duck, explain this behavior."

"Beg pardon, Sir, but I'm a Great Western Engine. We Great Western Engines do our work without fuss, but we are *not* ordered about by other engines. You, Sir, are our Controller. We will of course move if you order us, but begging your pardon, Sir, Percy and I would be glad if you would inform these—er—engines that we only take orders from you."

The three big engines hissed angrily.

"Silence!" snapped Sir Topham Hatt. "Percy and Duck, I am pleased with your work today, but *not* with your behavior tonight. You have caused a disturbance."

Gordon, Henry, and James snickered. They stopped suddenly when Sir Topham Hatt turned on them. "As for you," he thundered, "you've been worse. You made the disturbance. Duck is quite right. This is my railway, and I give the orders."

When Percy went away, Duck was left to manage alone.

He did so . . . easily!

Percy and Harold

Percy worked hard at the harbor. Toby helped, but sometimes the loads of stone were too heavy, and Percy had to fetch them for himself. Then he would push the freight cars along the wharf to where the workmen needed the stone for their building.

An airfield was close by, and Percy heard the airplanes zooming overhead all day. The noisiest of all

was a helicopter, which hovered, buzzing like an angry bee.

"Stupid thing!" said Percy. "Why can't it go and buzz somewhere else?"

One day, Percy stopped near the airfield. The helicopter was standing quite close.

"Hullo!" said Percy. "Who are you?"

"I'm Harold. Who are you?"

"I'm Percy. What whirly great arms you've got."

"They're nice arms," said Harold, offended. "I can hover like a bird. Don't you wish *you* could hover?"

"Certainly not; I like my rails, thank you."

"I think railways are slow," said Harold in a bored voice. "They're not much use and quite out of date." He whirled his arms and buzzed away.

Percy found Toby at the Top Station arranging freight cars.

"I say, Toby," he burst out, "that Harold, that stuck-up whirlybird thing, says I'm slow and out of date. Just let him wait, I'll show him!"

He collected his freight cars and started off, still fuming.

Soon, above the clatter of the freight cars, they heard a familiar buzzing.

"Percy," whispered his Driver, "there's Harold. He's not far ahead. Let's race him."

"Yes, let's," said Percy excitedly, and quickly gathering speed, he shot off down the line.

The Guard's wife had given him a thermos of tea. He had just poured out a cup when the van lurched, and he spilled it down his uniform. He wiped up the mess with his handkerchief and staggered to the front platform.

Percy was pounding along, and the freight cars

screamed and swayed while the van rolled and pitched like a ship at sea.

"Well, I'll be ding-dong-danged!" said the Guard.

Then he saw Harold buzzing alongside and understood.

"Go on, Percy!" he yelled. "You're gaining."

Percy had never been allowed to run fast before; he was having the time of his life!

"Hurry! Hurry! Hurry!" he panted to the freight cars.

"We—don't—want—to; we—don't—want—to," they grumbled, but it was no use. Percy was bucketing along with flying wheels, and Harold was high and alongside.

The Fireman shoveled for dear life, while the Driver was so excited he could hardly keep still.

"Well done, Percy," he shouted, "we're gaining! We're going ahead! Oh, good boy, good boy!"

Far ahead, a "distant" signal warned them that the wharf was near. They shut off steam and Percy whistled, "*Peep, peep, peep,* brakes, Guard, please." Using Percy's brakes, too, the Driver carefully checked the train's headlong speed. They rolled under the Main Line and halted smoothly on the wharf.

"Oh, dear!" groaned Percy. "I'm sure we've lost."

The Fireman scrambled to the cab roof. "We've won! We've won!" he shouted, and nearly fell off in his excitement.

"Harold's still hovering. He's looking for a place to land!"

"Listen, boys!" the Fireman called. "Here's a song for Percy."

Said Harold the Helicopter to our Percy, "You are slow!
Your railway is out of date and not much use, you know."
But Percy, with his stone cars,
    did the trip in record time;
And we beat that helicopter
        on Our Old Branch
            Line.

The Driver and Guard soon caught the tune, and so did the workmen on the wharf.

Percy loved it. "Oh, thank you!" he said. He liked the last line best of all.

Percy's Promise

A mob of excited children poured out of Annie and Clarabel one morning and raced down to the beach.

"They're the Vicar's Sunday School," explained Thomas. "I'm busy this evening, but the Station Master says I can ask you to take them home."

"Of course I will," promised Percy.

The children had a lovely day. But at teatime it got very hot. Dark clouds loomed overhead. Then came lightning, thunder, and rain. The children only just managed to reach shelter before the deluge began.

Annie and Clarabel stood at the platform. The children scrambled in.

"Can we go home, please, Station Master?" asked the Vicar.

The Station Master called Percy. "Take the children home quickly, please," he ordered.

The rain streamed down Percy's boiler. "Ugh!" He shivered and thought of his nice dry Shed. Then he remembered.

"A promise is a promise," he told himself, "so here goes."

His Driver was anxious. The river was rising fast. It foamed and swirled fiercely, threatening to flood the country any minute.

The rain beat in Percy's face. "I wish I could see, I wish I could see," he complained.

They came down a hill and found themselves in water. "Oooh, my wheels!" shivered Percy. "It's cold!" But he struggled on.

"*Oooooooooooooshshshshshsh!*" he hissed. "It's sloshing my fire."

They stopped and backed up the coaches and waited while the Guard found a telephone.

He returned, looking gloomy.

"We couldn't go back if we wanted," he said. "The bridge near the junction is down."

The Fireman went to the Guard's van carrying a hatchet.

"Hullo!" said the Guard. "You look fierce."

"I want some dry wood for Percy's fire, please."

They broke up some boxes, but that did not satisfy

the Fireman. "I'll need some of your floorboards," he said.

"What! My nice floor," grumbled the Guard. "I only swept it this morning." But he found a hatchet and helped.

Soon they had plenty of wood stored in Percy's bunker. His fire burned well now. He felt warm and comfortable again.

"Buzzzzzzzzzzzzzzzzzz! Buzzzzzzzzzzzzzzzzzz! Buzzzzzzzzzzzzzzzzzz!"

"Oh, dear!" thought Percy sadly. "Harold's come to laugh at me."

Bump! Something thudded on Percy's boiler. "Ow!" he exclaimed in a muffled voice. "That's really too bad! He needn't *throw* things."

His Driver unwound a parachute from Percy's indignant front.

"Harold isn't throwing things at you," he laughed. "He's dropping hot drinks for us."

They all had a drink of cocoa and felt better.

Percy had steam up now. "*Peep, peep!* Thank you, Harold!" he whistled. "Come on, let's go."

The water lapped his wheels. "Ugh!" He shivered. It crept up and up and up. It reached his ash pan, then it sloshed at his fire.

"Oooooooooooooooshshshshshshshshshshsh!"

Percy was losing steam, but he plunged bravely on. "I promised," he panted, "I promised."

They piled his fire high with wood and managed to keep him steaming.

"I *must* do it," he gasped, "I must, I must, I must."

He made a last great effort and stood, exhausted but

triumphant, on rails which were clear of the flood.

He rested to get steam back, then brought the train home.

"Three cheers for Percy!" called the Vicar, and the children nearly raised the roof!

Sir Topham Hatt arrived in Harold. First he thanked the men. "Harold told me you were—er—great, Percy. He says he can beat you at some things . . ."

Percy snorted.

". . . but *not* at being a submarine." He chuckled. "I don't know what you've both been playing at, and I won't ask! But I do know that you're a Really Useful Engine."

"Oh, Sir!" whispered Percy happily.

The Eight Famous Engines

The Eight Famous Engines

THE REV. W. AWDRY

with illustrations by

JOHN T. KENNEY

DEAR FRIENDS,

Sir Topham Hatt's engines are now quite famous. They have been on the radio and had many other adventures. But he had another plan, too, for his engines, and this book will tell you what it was.

THE AUTHOR

Percy Takes the Plunge

Sometimes Percy takes stone freight cars full of stones to the other end of the line. There he meets engines from the Other Railway.

One day, Henry wanted to rest in the Shed, but Percy was talking to some tank engines.

". . . It was raining hard. Water swirled under my boiler. I couldn't see where I was going, but I struggled on."

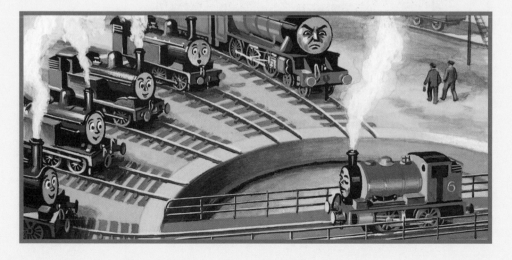

"Ooooh, Percy, you *are* brave."

"Well," said Percy modestly, "it wasn't anything really. Water's nothing to an engine with determination."

"Tell us more, Percy," said the engines.

"What are you engines doing here?" hissed Henry. "This Shed is for Sir Topham Hatt's engines. Go away. Silly things," Henry snorted.

"They're not silly." Percy had been enjoying himself.

He was cross because Henry had sent them away.

"They are silly, and so are you. 'Water's nothing to an engine with determination.' Pah!"

"Anyway," said cheeky Percy, "I'm not afraid of water. I like it." He ran away singing,

"Once an engine attached to a train
Was afraid of a few drops of rain . . ."

Percy arrived home feeling pleased with himself. "Silly old Henry," he chuckled.

Later, Thomas and Percy were at the wharf. There was a sign. It said DANGER.

"We mustn't go past it," he said. "That's orders."

"Why?"

" 'DANGER' means falling down something," said Thomas. "I went past 'DANGER' once and fell down a mine."

Percy looked beyond the sign. "I can't see a mine," he said.

He didn't know that the foundations of the wharf had sunk and the rails now sloped downwards to the sea.

"Silly sign!" said Percy. For days and days, he tried to sidle past it, but his Driver stopped him every time.

"No, you don't," he would say.

Then Percy made a plan.

One day at the Top Station, he whispered to the freight cars, "Will you give me a bump when we get to the wharf?"

The freight cars were surprised. They had never been asked to bump an engine before. They giggled and chattered about it the whole way down.

"Whoa, Percy! Whoa!" said his Driver, and Percy slowed down obediently at the distant signal.

"Driver doesn't know my plan," he chuckled.

"On! On! On!" laughed the freight cars.

Percy thought they were helping. "I'll pretend to stop at

the station, but the freight cars will push me past the sign. Then I'll make them stop. I can do that whenever I like."

If Percy hadn't been so conceited, he would never have been so silly. Every wise engine knows that you cannot trust freight cars.

They reached the station, and Percy's brakes groaned. That was the signal for the freight cars.

"Go on! Go on!" they yelled, and surged forward together.

They gave Percy a fearful bump and knocked his Driver and Fireman off the footplate.

"Ow!" said Percy, sliding past the sign.

The day was misty. The rails were slippery. His wheels wouldn't grip.

Percy was frantic. "That's enough!" he hissed.

But it was too late. Once on the slope, he tobogganed helplessly down, crashed through the buffers, and slithered into the sea.

"You are a very disobedient engine."

Percy knew that voice. He groaned.

The Foreman had borrowed a small boat and rowed Sir Topham Hatt round.

"Please, Sir, get me out, Sir. I'm truly sorry, Sir."

"No, Percy, we cannot do that till high tide. I hope it will teach you to obey orders."

"Yes, Sir." Percy shivered miserably. He was cold. Fish were playing hide-and-seek through his wheels. The tide rose higher and higher.

He was feeling his position more and more deeply every minute.

It was nearly dark when they brought floating cranes, cleared away the freight cars, and lifted Percy out.

He was too cold and stiff to move by himself, so he was sent to the Works the next day on Henry's goods

train.

"Well! Well! Well!" chuckled Henry. "Did you like the water?"

"No."

"I *am* surprised. You need more determination, Percy. 'Water's nothing to an engine with determination,' you know. Perhaps you will like it better next time."

But Percy is quite determined that there won't be a "next time."

Gordon Goes Foreign

Lots of people travel to the Big Station at the end of the line. Engines from the Other Railway sometimes pull their trains. These engines stay the night and go home the next day.

Gordon was talking one day to one of these.

"When I was young and green," he said, "I remember going to London. Do you know the place? The station's called King's Cross."

"King's Cross!" snorted the engine. "London's Euston. Everybody knows that."

"Rubbish!" said Duck. "London's Paddington. I *know*. I worked there."

They argued till they went to sleep. They argued when they woke up. They were still arguing when the other engine went away.

"Stupid thing," said Gordon crossly. "I've no patience."

"Stupid yourself," said Duck. "London's Paddington, PADDINGTON, do you hear?"

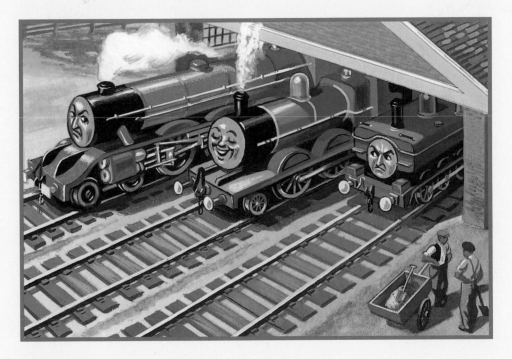

"Stop arguing," James broke in, "you make me tired. You're both agreed about something anyway."

"What's that?"

"London's not Euston," laughed James. "Now be quiet!"

Gordon rolled away still grumbling. "I'm sure it's King's Cross. I'll go and prove it."

But that was easier said than done.

London lay beyond the Big Station at the other end of the line. Gordon had to stop there. Another engine then took his train.

"If I didn't stop," he thought, "I could go to London." One day, he ran right through the station. Another time, he tried to start before the Fireman could uncouple the coaches. He tried all sorts of tricks, but it was no good. His Driver checked him every time.

"Oh, dear!" he thought sadly. "I'll never get there."

One day, he pulled the Express to the station, as usual. His Fireman uncoupled the coaches, and he ran onto his siding to wait till it was time to go home.

The coaches waited and waited at the platform, but their engine didn't come.

A porter ran across and spoke to Gordon's Driver.

"The Inspector's on the platform. He wants to see you."

The Driver climbed down from the cab and walked over to the station. He came back in a few minutes, looking excited.

"Hullo!" said the Fireman. "What's happened?"

"The engine for the Express turned over when it was coming out of the Yard. Nothing else can come in or out. They want us to take the train to London. I said we would, if Sir Topham Hatt agreed. They telephoned, and he said we could do it. How's that?"

"Fine," said the Fireman. "We'll show them what Sir Topham Hatt's engines can do."

"Come on!" said Gordon. "Let's go." He rolled quickly over the crossings and backed onto the train.

It was only a few minutes before the Guard blew his whistle, but Gordon thought it was ages!

"COME ON! COME ON!" he puffed to the coaches. "Comeoncomeoncomeon!"

"We're going to town, we're going to town," sang the coaches, slowly at first, then faster and faster.

Gordon found that London was a long way away. "Never mind," he said, "I like a good long run to stretch my wheels."

But all the same he was glad when London came into view.

Sir Topham Hatt came into his office the next morning. He looked at the letters on his desk. One had a London postmark.

"I wonder how Gordon's getting on," he said.

The Station Master knocked and came in. He looked excited.

"Excuse me, Sir, have you seen the news?"

"Not yet. Why?"

"Just look at this, Sir."

Sir Topham Hatt took the newspaper. "Good gracious me!" he said. "There's Gordon. Headlines, too! 'FAMOUS ENGINE AT LONDON STATION. POLICE CALLED TO CONTROL CROWDS.' "

Sir Topham Hatt read on, absorbed.

Gordon returned the next day. Sir Topham Hatt spoke to his Driver and Fireman.

"I see you had a good welcome in London."

"We certainly did, Sir! We signed autographs till our arms ached, and Gordon had his photograph taken from so many directions at once that he didn't know which way to look!"

"Good!" smiled Sir Topham Hatt. "I expect he enjoyed himself. Didn't you, Gordon?"

"No, Sir, I didn't."

"Why ever not?"

"London's all wrong," answered Gordon sadly. "They've changed it. It isn't King's Cross anymore. It's St. Pancras."

Double Header

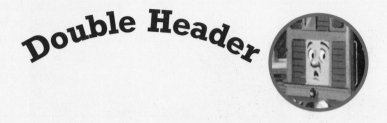

S ir Topham Hatt gave Gordon a rest when he came
back from London. He told James to do Gordon's
work. James got very conceited about it.

"You know, little Toby," he said one day, "I'm an
important engine now. Everybody knows it. They come
in crowds to see me flash by. The heaviest train makes

424

no difference. I'm as regular as clockwork. They all set their watches by me. Never late, always on time, that's me."

"Says you," replied Toby cheekily.

Toby was out on the Main Line. Sir Topham Hatt had sent him to the Works. His parts were worn. They clanked as he trundled along.

He was enjoying his journey. He was a little engine, and his tanks didn't hold much water, so he often had to stop for a drink. He had small wheels, too, and he couldn't go fast.

"Never mind," he thought, "the Signalmen all know

me. They'll give me plenty of time."

But a new Signalman had come to one of the stations.

Toby had wanted to take Henrietta, but Sir Topham Hatt had said, "No! What would the passengers do without her?"

He wondered if Henrietta was lonely. Percy had promised to look after her, but Toby couldn't help worrying. "Percy doesn't understand her like I do," he said.

He felt thirsty and tired; he had come a long way.

He saw a "yield" signal. "Good," he thought, "now I

can have a nice drink and rest in a siding till James has gone by."

Toby's Driver thought so, too. They stopped by the water tower. His Fireman jumped out and put the hose in his tank.

Toby was enjoying his drink when the Signalman came up. Toby had never seen him before.

"No time for that," said the Signalman. "We must clear the road for the Express."

"Right," said the Driver. "We'll wait in the siding."

"No good," said the Signalman, "it's full of freight

cars. You'll have to hurry to the next station. They've got plenty of room for you there."

Poor Toby clanked sadly away. "I must hurry! I must hurry!" he panted.

But hurrying used a lot of water, and his tanks were soon empty.

They lowered his fire and struggled on, but he soon ran out of steam and stood marooned on the Main Line far away from the next station.

The Fireman walked back. He put flares on the line to warn James and his Driver; then he hurried along the shoulder.

"I'll tell that Signalman something," he said grimly.

James was fuming when Toby's Fireman arrived and explained what had happened.

"My fault," said the Signalman. "I didn't understand about Toby."

"Now, James," said his Driver, "you'll have to push him."

"What, me?" snorted James. "*Me* push Toby *and* pull my train?"

"Yes, you."

"Shan't."

The Driver, the Firemen, the passengers, and the

Guard all said he was a bad engine.

"All right, all right," grumbled James. He came up behind Toby and gave him a bump.

"Get on, you!" he said crossly.

James' Driver made him push Toby all the way to the Works. "It serves you right for being cross," the Driver said to James.

James had to work very hard, and when he reached the Works, he felt exhausted.

Some little boys ran along the platform. "Look!" said one. "The Express *is* late. A double header, too.

Do you know what I think? I think," he went on, "that James couldn't pull the train, so Toby had to help him."

"Grrr!" said James, and disappeared in a cloud of steam.

Oone evening, Thomas brought his last train to the junction. He went for a drink.

"I'm going to the Big Station," he said to Percy and Toby.

"So are we," they answered.

"Do you know," Percy went on, "I think something's up."

Toby looked at the sky. "Where?"

"Down here, silly," laughed Thomas.

"How?" asked Toby reasonably. "Can something be up when it's down?"

"Look!" said Thomas excitedly. "Look!"

Seven engines from the Other Railway were coming along the line.

"Hullo, Jinty!" whistled Percy. "Hullo, Pug!

"They're friends of mine," he explained. "I don't know the others."

Jinty and Pug whistled cheerfully as they puffed through the station.

"What *is* all this?" asked Thomas.

"Sir Topham Hatt's got a plan," answered his Driver, "and he's going to tell it to us. Come on."

So they followed Thomas to the Big Station at the end of the line, where all the engines had gone.

Sir Topham Hatt was waiting for them there.

"The people of England," he said, "read about us in storybooks, but they do not think that we are real. . . ."

"Shame!" squeaked Percy. Sir Topham Hatt glared. Percy subsided.

"So," he continued, "I am taking my engines to England to show them."

"Hooray! Hooray!" the engines whistled.

Sir Topham Hatt held his ears. "Silence!" he bellowed. "We start the day after tomorrow at 8 a.m. Meanwhile, as these engines have kindly come from the Other Railway to take your place, you will show them your work tomorrow."

The next day—as Annie and Clarabel were going to England, too—Thomas and Jinty practiced with some other coaches.

Thomas was excited. He began boasting about his race with Bertie. "I *whoosh*ed through the tunnel and stopped an inch from the buffers. Like this!" —CRASH!—

The buffers broke.

No one was hurt, but Thomas' front was badly bent.

They telephoned Sir Topham Hatt. "I'll send up some men," he said, "but if they can't mend Thomas in time, we'll go to England without him."

The next morning, the engines waited at the junction. Toby and Percy were each on a flatbed, and Duck had pushed them into place behind Edward.

Henrietta stood on a siding. Sir Topham Hatt had called her a "curiosity." "I wouldn't dream of leaving you behind," he said. "I'll fit you up as my private coach." She felt very grand.

Gordon, James, and Henry were in front. They whistled impatiently.

Sir Topham Hatt paced the platform. He looked at

his watch. "One minute more," he said, turning to the Guard.

"*Peep, peep, peeep!*" whistled Thomas, and panted into the station.

Annie and Clarabel twittered anxiously. "We hope we're not late; it isn't quite eight."

"Thomas," said Sir Topham Hatt sternly, "I am most displeased with you. You nearly upset my arrangements."

Thomas, abashed, arranged himself and the coaches

behind Duck without saying a word!

Sir Topham Hatt climbed into Henrietta. The Guard blew his whistle and waved his flag.

The engines whistled, "Look out, England, here we come!" And the cavalcade puffed off.

Once there, the engines stood side by side in a big airy shed. Hundreds of people came to see them and climbed in and out of their cabs every day.

The engines liked it at first, but presently felt very bored and were glad when it was time to go.

When they got home, the people along their line put flags out and cheered. "We are glad to see you," they said. "Those others did their best, but they don't know our ways. Nothing anywhere can compare with Sir Topham Hatt's engines."

Duck and the Diesel Engine

Duck and the Diesel Engine

THE REV. W. AWDRY

with illustrations by

JOHN T. KENNEY

DEAR FRIENDS,

We have had two visitors to our railway. One of these, City of Truro, is a very famous engine. We were sorry when we had to say goodbye to him.

The other visitor was different. "I do not believe," writes Sir Topham Hatt, "that all diesels are troublesome, but this one upset our engines and made Duck very unhappy."

THE AUTHOR

Domeless Engines

A Special Train arrived one day, and Sir Topham Hatt welcomed the passengers. They looked at everything in the Yard and photographed the engines. Duck's Driver let some of them ride in his cab.

"They're the Railway Society," his Driver explained. "They've come to see us. Their engine's called 'City of

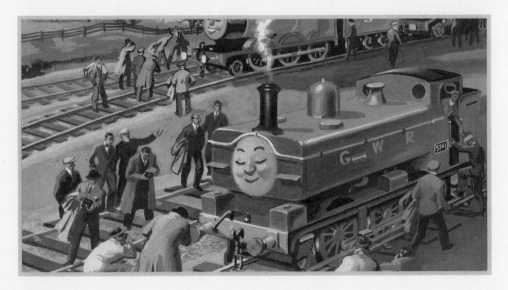

Truro.' He was the first to go 100 miles an hour. Let's get finished, then we can go and talk to him."

"Oh!" said Duck, awed. "He's too famous to notice me."

"Rubbish!" smiled his Driver. "Come on."

Duck found City of Truro at the coaling station.

"May I talk to you?" he asked shyly.

"Of course," smiled the famous engine. "I see you are one of *us*."

"I try to teach them *our* ways," said Duck modestly.

"All shipshape and Swindon-fashion. That's right."

"Please, could you tell me how you beat the South Western?"

So City of Truro told Duck all about his famous
run from Plymouth to Bristol more than fifty years
ago. They were soon firm friends and talked "Great
Western" till late at night.

City of Truro left early next morning.

"Good riddance!" grumbled Gordon. "Chattering
all night, keeping important engines awake! Who *is*
he, anyway?"

"He's City of Truro. He's famous."

"As famous as me? Nonsense!"

"He's famouser than you. He went 100 miles an
hour before you were drawn or thought of."

"So he says, but I didn't like his looks. *He's got no dome,*" said Gordon darkly. "Never trust domeless engines, they're not respectable.

"I never boast," Gordon continued modestly, "but 100 miles an hour would be easy for me. Goodbye!"

Presently, Duck took some freight cars to Edward's station. He was cross and it was lucky for the freight cars that they tried no tricks.

"Hullo!" called Edward. "The famous City of Truro came through this morning. He whistled to me. Wasn't he kind?"

"He's the finest engine in the world," said Duck. He told Edward about City of Truro and what Gordon had said.

"Don't take any notice," soothed Edward. "He's just jealous. He thinks no engine should be famous but him. Look! He's coming now."

Gordon's boiler seemed to have swollen larger than ever. He was running very fast. He swayed up and down and from side to side as his wheels pounded the rails.

"He did it! I'll do it! He did it! I'll do it!" he panted. His train rocketed past and was gone.

Edward chuckled and winked at Duck. "Gordon's

trying to do a 'City of Truro,' " he said.

Duck was still cross. "I should think he'll knock himself to bits," he snorted. "I heard something rattle as he went through."

Gordon's Driver eased him off. "Steady, boy!" he said. "We aren't running a race."

"We are, too," said Gordon, but he said it to himself.

"I've never known him to ride so roughly before," remarked his Driver.

His Fireman grabbed the brake handle to steady himself. "He's giving himself a hammering, and no mistake."

Soon Gordon began to feel a little queer. "The top of my boiler seems funny," he thought. "It's just as if something were loose. I'd better go slower."

But by then, it was too late!

They met the wind on the viaduct. It wasn't just a gentle wind, nor was it a hard steady wind. It was a

teasing wind which blew suddenly in hard puffs and caught you unawares.

Gordon thought it wanted to push him off the bridge. "No you don't!" he said firmly.

But the wind had other ideas. It curled round his boiler, crept under his loose dome, and lifted it off and away into the valley below. It fell on the rocks with a clang.

Gordon was most uncomfortable. He felt cold where his dome wasn't, and, besides, people laughed at him as he passed.

At the Big Station, he tried to *wheeeesh* them away,

but they crowded round no matter what he did.

On the way back, Gordon wanted his Driver to stop and find his dome, and was very cross when he wouldn't.

He hoped the Shed would be empty, but all the engines were there, waiting.

"Never trust domeless engines," said a voice. "They aren't respectable."

City of Truro's visit made Duck very proud of being Great Western. He talked endlessly about it. But he worked hard, too, and made everything go like clockwork.

The freight cars behaved well, the coaches were ready on time, and the passengers even stopped

grumbling!

But the engines didn't like having to bustle about. "There are two ways of doing this," Duck told them, "the Great Western way or the wrong way. I'm Great Western and . . ."

"Don't we know it!" they groaned. They were glad when a visitor came.

The visitor purred smoothly towards them. Sir Topham Hatt climbed down. "Here is Diesel," he said.

"I have agreed to give him a trial. He needs to learn. Please teach him, Duck."

"Good morning," purred Diesel in an oily voice. "Pleased to meet you, Duck. Is that James?—*and* Henry?—*and* Gordon, too? I am delighted to meet such famous engines." And he purred towards them.

The silly engines were flattered. "He has very good manners," they murmured. "We are pleased to have him in our Yard."

Duck had his doubts.

"Come on!" he said shortly.

"Ah! Yes!" said Diesel. "The Yard, of course. Excuse me, engines." And he purred after Duck, talking hard. "Your worthy boss . . ."

"Sir Topham Hatt to you," ordered Duck.

Diesel looked hurt.

"Your worthy Sir Topham Hatt thinks I need to learn. He is mistaken. We diesels don't need to learn. We know everything. We come to a yard and improve it. We are revolutionary."

"Oh!" said Duck. "If you're revo–thingummy, perhaps you would collect my freight cars while I fetch Gordon's coaches."

Diesel, delighted to show off, purred away. With much banging and clashing, he collected a row of freight cars. Duck left Gordon's coaches in the station and came back.

Diesel was now trying to take some freight cars

from a siding nearby. They were old and empty. Clearly, they had not been touched for a long time.

Their brakes would not come off properly. Diesel found them hard to move.

Pull—Push—Backwards—Forwards. "Oheeeer! Oheeeer!" the freight cars groaned. "We can't! We *won't*!"

Duck watched the operation with interest.

Diesel lost patience. *"GrrrrrRRRRRrrrrrRRRRR!"* he roared, and gave a great heave. The freight cars jerked forward.

"Oher! Oher!" they screamed. "We *can't*! We *WON'T*!" Some of their brakes broke, and the gear

hanging down bumped on the rails and sleepers.

"WE CAN'T! WE WON'T! Aaaaah!" Their trailing brakes caught in the switches and locked themselves solid.

"GrrrrrRRRRRrrrrrRRRRRrrrrrRRRR!" roared Diesel. A rusty coupling broke, and he shot forward suddenly by himself.

"Ho! Ho! Ho!" chuckled Duck.

Diesel recovered and tried to push the freight cars back, but they wouldn't move, and he had to give up. Duck ran quietly round to where the other freight cars all stood in line. "Thank you for arranging these, Diesel," he said. "I must go now."

"Don't you want this lot?"

"No, thank you."

Diesel gulped. "And I've taken all this trouble," he almost shrieked. "Why didn't you tell me?"

"You never asked me. Besides," said Duck innocently, "you were having such fun being revo-whatever-it-was-you-said. Goodbye."

Diesel had to help the workmen clear the mess. He hated it. All the freight cars and coaches were

laughing. Presently, he heard them sing. Their song grew louder and louder, and soon it echoed through the Yard.

Freight cars waiting in the Yard;
tackling them with ease'll
"Show the world what I can do,"
gaily boasts the Diesel.
In and out, he creeps about
like a big black weasel.
When he pulls the wrong ones out—
Pop goes the Diesel!

"Grrrrr!" he growled, and scuttling away, sulked in the Shed.

Dirty Work

When Duck returned and heard the freight cars singing, he was horrified. "Be quiet!" he ordered and bumped them hard. "I'm sorry our freight cars were rude to you, Diesel," he said.

Diesel was still furious. "It's all your fault. You made them laugh at me," he complained.

"Nonsense," said Henry. "Duck would never do that. We engines have our differences, but we *never* talk about them to freight cars. That would be des—des . . ."

"Disgraceful!" said Gordon.

"Disgusting!" put in James.

"Despicable!" finished Henry.

Diesel hated Duck. He wanted him to be sent away. So he made a plan.

Next day, he spoke to the freight cars. "I see you like jokes," he said in his oily voice. "You made a good joke about me yesterday. I laughed and laughed. Duck

told me one about Gordon. I'll whisper it . . . don't
tell Gordon I told you." And he sniggered away.

"Haw! Haw! Haw!" guffawed the freight cars.
"Gordon will be cross with Duck when he knows.
Let's tell him and pay Duck back for bumping us."

Diesel went to all the sidings, and in each he told
different stories. He said Duck had told them to him.
This was untrue, but the freight cars didn't know.

They laughed rudely at the engines as they went by,
and soon Gordon, Henry, and James found out why.

"Disgraceful!" said Gordon.

"Disgusting!" said James.

"Despicable!" said
Henry. "We cannot
allow it."

They consulted
together. "Yes," they
said, "he did it to us.
We'll do it to him and see
how *he* likes it."

Duck was tired out. The freight cars had been

cheeky and troublesome. He had to work hard to make them behave. He wanted a rest in the Shed.

"*Hooooooooosh!* KEEP OUT!" The three engines barred his way, and Diesel lurked behind.

"Stop fooling," said Duck. "I'm tired."

"So are we," hissed the engines. "We are tired of *you*. We like Diesel. We don't like you. You tell tales about us to freight cars."

"I don't."

"You do."

"I don't."

"You do."

Sir Topham Hatt came to stop the noise.

"Duck called me a 'galloping sausage,'" spluttered Gordon.

"... rusty red scrap iron," hissed James.

"... I'm 'old square wheels,'" fumed Henry.

"Well, Duck?"

Duck considered. "I only wish, Sir," he said, "that I'd thought of those names myself. If the dome fits ..."

"Ha! Ahem!" Sir Topham Hatt coughed.

"He made freight cars laugh at us," accused the engines.

Sir Topham Hatt recovered. "Did you, Duck?"

"Certainly not, Sir! No *steam* engine would be as mean as that."

"Now, Diesel, you heard what Duck said."

"I can't understand it, Sir. To think that Duck, of all

engines. . . I'm very grieved, Sir, but know nothing."

"I see."

Diesel squirmed and hoped he didn't.

"I am sorry, Duck," Sir Topham Hatt went on, "but you must go to Edward's station for a while. I know he will be glad to see you."

"Beg pardon, Sir, do you mean now?"

"Yes, please."

"As you wish, Sir." Duck trundled sadly away, while Diesel smirked with triumph in the darkness.

A Close Shave

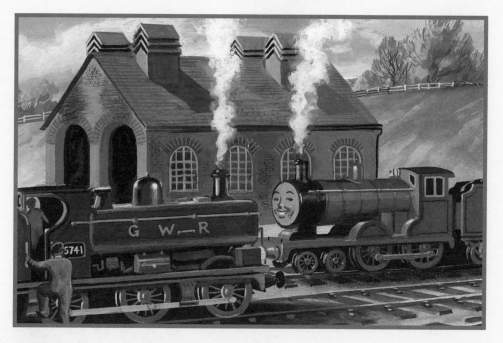

So Duck came to Edward's station.

"It's not fair," he complained. "Diesel has made Sir Topham Hatt and all the engines think I'm horrid."

Edward smiled. "I know you aren't," he said, "and so does Sir Topham Hatt. You wait and see."

Duck felt happier with Edward. He helped him with his freight cars and coaches, and sometimes he helped foreign engines by pushing their trains up the hill.

But Gordon, Henry, and James never spoke to him at all.

One day, he pushed behind a goods train and helped it to the top.

"*Peep, peep!* Goodbye!" he called, and rolled gently over the crossing to the other line. Duck loved coasting down the hill, running easily with the wind whistling past. He hummed a little tune.

* * *

"*Peeeeeep! Peeeeeep! Peeeeeep!*"

"That sounds like a Guard's whistle," he thought. "But we haven't a Guard."

His Driver heard it, too,

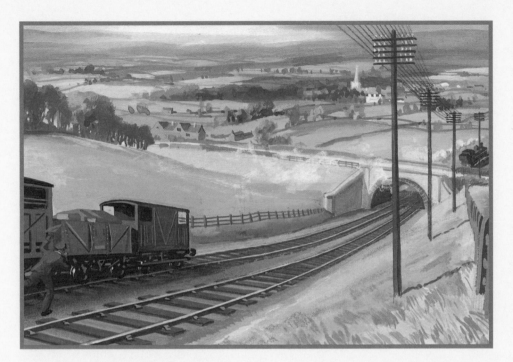

and looked back. "Hurry, Duck, hurry," he called urgently. "There's been a breakaway, some freight cars are chasing us."

There were twenty heavily loaded freight cars. "Hurrah! Hurrah! Hurrah!" they laughed. "We've broken away! We've broken away! We've broken away!" And before the Signalman could change the switches, they followed Duck onto the down line.

"Chase him! Bump him! Throw him off the rails!" they yelled, and hurtled after Duck, bumping and

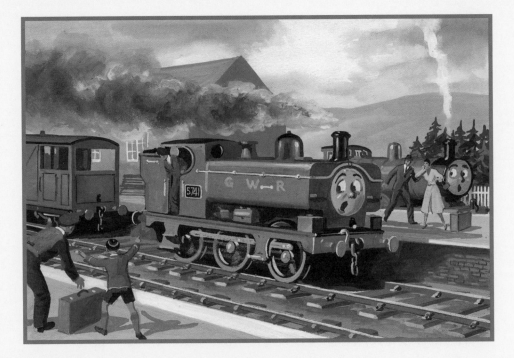

swaying with ever-increasing speed.

The Guard saved Duck. Though the freight cars had knocked the Guard off his van, he got up and ran behind, blowing his whistle to attract the Driver's attention.

"Now what?" asked the Fireman.

"As fast as we can," said the Driver grimly, "then they'll catch us gradually."

They raced through Edward's station, whistling furiously, but the freight cars caught them with a shuddering jar. The Fireman climbed back, and the van brakes came on with a scream.

Braking carefully, the Driver was gaining control.

"Another clear mile and we'll do it," he said.

They swept round a bend.

"Oh, glory! Look at that!"

A passenger train was just pulling out on the line from the station ahead.

The Driver leaped to his reverser. Hard over—Full steam—Whistle.

"It's up to you now, Duck," he said.

Duck put every ounce of weight and steam against the freight cars.

They felt his strength. "On! On!" they yelled, but Duck was holding them now.

"I must stop them. I *must*."

The station came nearer and nearer. The last coach cleared the platform.

"It's too late," Duck groaned, and shut his eyes.

He felt a sudden swerve and slid, shuddering and groaning along a siding.

A barber had set up shop in a wooden shed in the yard. He was shaving a customer.

There was a sliding, groaning crash, and part of the wall caved in.

The customer jumped nervously, but the barber

held him down. "It's only an engine," he said calmly, and went on lathering.

"Beg pardon, sir!" gasped Duck. "Excuse my intrusion."

"No. I won't," said the barber crossly. "You've frightened my customers and spoiled my new paint. I'll teach you." And he lathered Duck's face all over.

Poor Duck.

They were pulling the freight cars away when Sir Topham Hatt arrived. The barber was telling the

workmen what he thought.

"I do *not* like engines popping through my walls,"
he fumed. "They disturb my customers."

"I appreciate your feelings," said Sir Topham Hatt,
"and we'll gladly repair the damage. But you must
know that this engine and his crew have prevented
a serious accident. You and many others might have
been badly hurt."

Sir Topham Hatt paused impressively. "It was a very
close shave," he said.

"Oh!" said the barber. "Oh! Excuse me." He ran into his shop, fetched a basin of water, and washed Duck's face.

"I'm sorry, Duck," he said. "I didn't know you were being a brave engine."

"That's all right, sir," said Duck. "I didn't know that, either."

"You were very brave indeed," said Sir Topham Hatt kindly. "I'm proud of you. I shall tell City of Truro about you next time he comes."

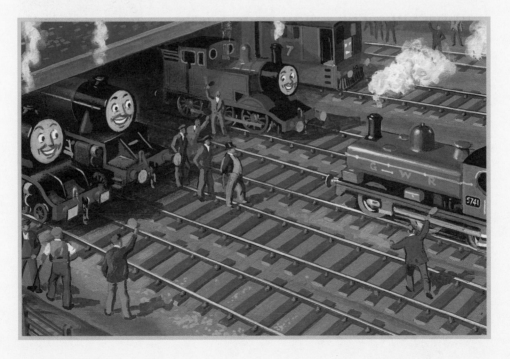

"Oh, Sir!" Duck felt happier than he had been for weeks.

"And now," said Sir Topham Hatt, "when you are mended, you are coming home."

"Home, Sir? Do you mean the Yard?"

"Of course."

"But, Sir, they don't like me. They like Diesel."

"Not now." Sir Topham Hatt smiled. "I never believed Diesel. After you went, he told lies about Henry, so I sent him packing. The engines are sorry and want you back."

So, when a few days later he came home shining with new paint, there was a really rousing welcome for Duck the Great Western Engine.

The Twin Engines

 "Hullo, Twins!"

 The Missing Coach

 Brake Van

 The Deputation

The Twin Engines

THE REV. W. AWDRY

with illustrations by

JOHN T. KENNEY

DEAR FRIENDS,

  Sir Topham Hatt has just been having a disturbing time! He ordered one goods engine from Scotland and was surprised to receive two!

  They had both lost their numbers and no one knew which was which. So he didn't know which engine to keep.

THE AUTHOR

"Hullo, Twins!"

More and more people traveled on Sir Topham Hatt's railway. More and more ships came to the harbors. Everyone had to work very hard indeed.

The freight cars complained bitterly; but then, freight cars always do, and no one takes much notice.

The coaches complained, too. No sooner had they arrived with one train than they had to go out again with fresh passengers on another.

"We don't know whether we're coming or going," they protested. "We feel *quite* distracted."

"No one can say," grumbled Henry, "that we're afraid of hard work, but . . ."

". . . we draw the line at goods trains," finished Gordon.

"Dirty freight cars, dirty sidings. Ugh!" put in James.

"What are you boiler-aching about?" asked Duck. "I remember on the Great Western . . ."

"That tin-pot railway . . ."

"Tin-pot indeed! Let me tell you . . ."

"Silence!" ordered a well-known voice. "Let me tell you that an engine for goods work will arrive from Scotland tomorrow."

The news was received with acclamation.

The next day, the Inspector brought news.

Sir Topham Hatt stared. "Did you say *two* engines, Inspector?"

"Yes, Sir."

"Then send the other back at once."

"Certainly, Sir, but which?"

Sir Topham Hatt stared again. "Engines have numbers, Inspector," he explained patiently. "We bought No. 57646. Send the other one back."

"Quite so, Sir, but there is a difficulty."

"What *do* you mean?"

"The two engines are exactly alike, Sir, and have no numbers. They say they lost them on the way."

Sir Topham Hatt seized his hat. "We'll soon settle that nonsense," he said grimly.

The two engines greeted him cheerfully.

"I hear you've lost your numbers," Sir Topham Hatt said. "How did that happen?"

"They may hae slyly slipped off, Sirr. Ye know hoo it is," the engines spoke in chorus.

"I know. Accidentally on purpose."

The twins looked pained. "Sirr! Ye wouldn' be thinkin' we lost them on purrpose?"

"I'm not so sure," said Sir Topham Hatt. "Now then, which of you is 57646?"

"That, Sirr, is just what we canna mind."

Sir Topham Hatt looked at their solemn faces.
He turned away. He seemed to have difficulty with
his own.

He swung round again. "What
are your names?"

"Donal an' Douggie,
Sirr."

"Good!" he said. "Then
your Controller can tell me
which of you is which."

"Och! Ye won't get much
help fae him, Sirr."

"Why?"

"He doesn't know oor names, Sirr. How could he?
We only gae ourselves names when we lost oor
nummers."

"One of you," said Sir Topham Hatt, "is playing
truant. I shall find him out and send him home.
Inspector," he ordered, "give these engines numbers
and set them to work."

He walked sternly away.

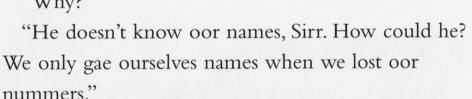

The Missing Coach

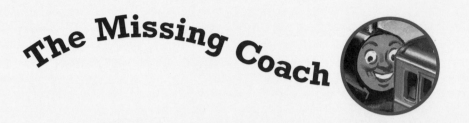

Soon, workmen came to give the twins their numbers. Donald was 9 and Douglas 10. When the men went away, they were left alone in the Shed.

"Ye may hae noticed, Douggie, that yon painters forgot somethin'."

"What did they forget?"

"They painted bran' new nummers on oor tenders, but they put none on uz." Donald winked broadly at his twin.

"Ye mean," grinned Douglas, "that we can . . ."

"Just that," chuckled Donald. "Keep it down. Here's the Inspector."

"Now 9 and 10," smiled the Inspector, "here's Duck. He'll show you round before you start work."

The twins enjoyed themselves and were soon friends with Duck. They didn't mind what they did. They tackled goods trains and coaches easily, for, once the twins had shunted them, freight cars knew better than to try any tricks.

"We like it fine here," said Donald.

"That's good," smiled Duck, "but take my tip, watch

out for Gordon, Henry, and James. They're sure to try some nonsense."

"Don' worry yersel," chuckled Douglas. "We'll soon settle them."

Donald and Douglas had deep-toned whistles.

"They sound like buses," said Gordon.

"Or ships," sniggered Henry.

"Tugboat Annie!" laughed Gordon. "Ha! Ha!"

Donald and Douglas cruised quietly up, one on each side. "Ye wouldn' be makin' fun o' us, would ye noo?" asked Donald.

Gordon and Henry jumped. They glanced nervously from side to side.

"Er, no," said Gordon.

"No, no, certainly not," said Henry.

"That's fine," said Douglas. "Noo just mind the both o' ye, and keep it that way."

And that was the way Gordon and Henry kept it!

Every day, punctually at 3:30, Gordon steams in with the Express. It is called the "Wild Nor' Wester," and it is full of people from England, Wales, and Scotland. There is also a Special Coach for passengers traveling to places on Thomas' Branch Line.

When the other coaches are taken away empty, engines have to remember to shunt the Special Coach to the bay platform. It does not wait there long.

Thomas, with Annie and Clarabel, comes hurrying from the junction to fetch it. Thomas is very proud of his Special Coach.

One afternoon, Douglas helped Duck in the Yard while Donald waited to take a goods train to the other end of the line. As Duck was busy arranging Donald's freight cars, Douglas offered to take away Gordon's coaches.

Douglas was enjoying himself, when an awful thought struck him. "I hope Sir Topham Hatt doesn' find oot I shouldn' be here. I couldn' abide goin' back." He worried so much over this that he forgot about Thomas' Special Coach.

He pushed it with the others into the carriage siding, then ambled along to join Donald at the water column. As he went, Thomas scampered by, whistling cheerfully.

Soon Thomas came fussing. "Where's my coach?"

"Cooch?" asked Donald. "What cooch?"

"My Special Coach that Gordon brings for me. It's gone. I must find it." He bustled away.

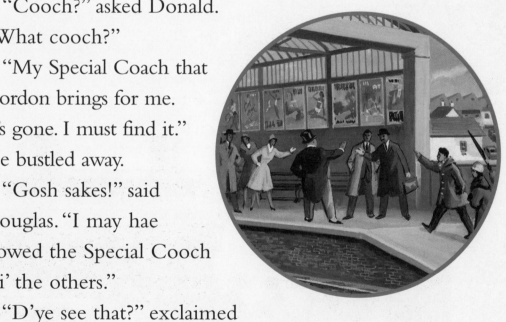

"Gosh sakes!" said Douglas. "I may hae stowed the Special Cooch wi' the others."

"D'ye see that?" exclaimed Donald's Driver. A mob of angry passengers erupted from the siding. "They're complainin' to Sir Topham Hatt. He'll be comin' here next."

"Now listen," said Douglas' Driver. "We'll change tenders. Then away wi' ye, Donal, and take those goods. Don' worry aboot us. Quick noo! Do as I say."

Sir Topham Hatt and three passengers walked towards them, but Donald, with Douglas' tender (10), was out and away with the goods before they came near. Douglas and his Driver waited with innocent expressions.

"Ah!" said Sir Topham Hatt. "No. 9, and why have you not taken the goods?"

"My tender is away, Sirr." The Driver showed him the tender, still uncoupled.

"I see, some defect, no doubt. Tell me, why did No. 10 leave so quickly?"

"Mebbe, Sirr," put in Douglas, "he saw ye comin' an' thought he was late."

"Hmm," said Sir Topham Hatt

He turned to the passengers. "Here, gentlemen, are the facts. No. 10 has been shunting the Yard. Your coach disappeared. We investigate. No. 10—er—disappears, too. You can draw your conclusions. Please accept my apologies. The matter will be investigated. Good afternoon, gentlemen."

Sir Topham Hatt watched them till they had climbed the station ramp. His shoulders twitched; he wiped his eyes. Douglas wondered if he was crying. He was not.

He swung round suddenly. "Douglas," he rapped, "why are you masquerading with Donald's tender?"

Brake Van

Sir Topham Hatt scolded both engines severely.

"There must be no more tricks," he said. "I shall be watching you both. I have to decide which of you is to stay." He strode away.

The twins looked glum. Neither wanted to stay without the other. They said so.

"Then what are we tae do?" wondered Douglas.

"Och!" said Donald. "Each of us be as good as the ither. Then he'll have tae keep us baith."

Their plan was good, but they had reckoned without a spiteful brake van.

The van had taken a dislike to Douglas. Things always went wrong when Douglas had to take it out. Then his trains were late and he was blamed. Douglas began to worry.

"Ye're a muckle nuisance," said Donald one day. "It's tae leave ye behind I'd be wantin'."

"You can't," said the van, "I'm essential."

"Och! Are ye?" Donald burst out. "Ye're nothin' but a screechin' an' a noise when all's said an' done. Spite Douggie, would ye? Take that."

"Oh! Oh! Oh!" cried the van.

"Quit yer whinin'," said Donald severely. "There's more comin' if ye misbehave."

The van behaved better after that. Douglas' trains were punctual, and the twins felt happier.

Then Donald had an accident. He backed into a siding. The rails were slippery. He couldn't stop in time

and crashed through the buffers into a signal box.

One moment, the Signalman was standing on the stairs; the next, he was sitting on the coal in Donald's tender. He was most annoyed.

"You clumsy great engine," he stormed. "Now you must stay there. You've jammed my switches. It serves you right for spoiling my nice new signal box."

Sir Topham Hatt was cross, too. "I am disappointed, Donald," he said. "I did not expect such—er—such clumsiness from you. I had decided to send Douglas back and keep you."

"I'm sorry, Sirr." But Donald didn't say what he was sorry for. We know, don't we?

"I should think so, too," Sir Topham Hatt went on indignantly. "You have upset my arrangements. It is most inconvenient. Now James will have to help with the goods work while you have your tender mended. James won't like that."

Sir Topham Hatt was right. James grumbled dreadfully.

"One would think," said Douglas, "that Donal had his accident on purrpose." He went on. "I heard tell aboot an engine an' some tar wagons."

Gordon and Henry chuckled.

"Shut up!" said James. "It's not funny."

"Weel, weel, weel!" said Douglas innocently. "Shairly, James, it wasna ye? Ye don' say!"

James didn't say. He was sulky the next morning and wouldn't steam properly. When at last he did start, he bumped the freight cars hard.

"He's cross," sniggered the spiteful brake van. "We'll try to make him crosser still!"

"Hold back!" whispered the van to the freight cars.

"Hold back!" giggled the freight cars to each other. James did his best, but he was exhausted when they reached Edward's station. Luckily Douglas was there.

"Help me up the hill, please," panted James.

"These freight cars are playing tricks."

"We'll show them," said Douglas grimly.

"ComeonComeonCOMEON," puffed James crossly.

"Get MOV-in', you! Get MOV-in', you!" puffed Douglas from behind.

Slowly but surely, the snorting engines forced the unwilling freight cars up the hill.

But James was losing steam. "I can't do it, I can't do it," he panted.

"LEAVE IT TAE ME! LEAVE IT TAE ME!" shouted Douglas. He pushed and he puffed so furiously that sparks leaped from his funnel.

"Ooer!" groaned the van. "I wish I'd never thought of this." It was squeezed between Douglas and the freight cars. "Go on! Go on!" it screamed, but they took no notice.

The Guard was anxious. "Go steady!" he yelled to Douglas. "The van's breaking."

It was too late. The Guard jumped as the van

collapsed. He landed safely on the side of the line.

"I might have known it would be Douglas!"

"I'm sorry, Sirr. Mebbe I was clumsy, but I *wouldn'* be beaten by yon tricksie van."

"I see," said Sir Topham Hatt.

Edward brought workmen to clear the mess.

"Douglas was grand, Sir," he said. "James had no steam left, but Douglas worked hard enough for three. I heard him from my yard."

"Two would have been enough," said Sir Topham Hatt dryly. "I want to be fair, Douglas," he went on. "I admire your determination, but . . . I don't know, I really don't know." He turned and walked thoughtfully away.

"He'll send us away for sure, Donal."

"I'm thinkin' ye're right there, Douggie. Luck's been agin us. An engine doesn' know what tae do for the best."

Snow came early that year. It was heavier than usual. It stayed, too, and choked the lines. Most engines hate snow. Donald and Douglas were used to it. They knew what to do. Their Drivers spoke to the Inspector, and they were soon coupled back to back, with a van between their tenders. Then, each with a snowplow on their fronts, they set to work.

They puffed busily backwards and forwards, patrolling the line. Generally, the snow slipped away easily, but sometimes they found deeper drifts.

Then they would charge them again and again,

snorting, slipping, puffing, panting, till they had forced their way through.

Presently, they came to a drift which was larger than most. They charged it, and were backing for another try. There was a feeble whistle; people waved and shouted.

"Heavans sakes, Donal, it's Henry! Don' worry yersel, Henry. Wait a bit. We'll have ye oot!"

* * *

Sir Topham Hatt was returning soon. The twins were glum. "He'll send us back for sure," they said.

"It's a shame!" sympathized Percy.

"A lot of nonsense about a signal box," grumbled

Gordon. "Too many of those, if you ask me."

"That brake van, too," put in James. "Good riddance. That's what I say."

"They were splendid in the snow," added Henry. "It isn't fair." They all agreed that something must be done, but none knew what.

One day, Percy talked to Edward about it.

"What you need," said Edward, "is a Deputation." He explained what that was.

Percy ran back quickly. "Edward says we need

a Depotstation," he told the others.

"Of course," said Gordon, "the question is . . ."

". . . What is a Desperation?" asked Henry.

"It's when engines tell Sir Topham Hatt something's wrong and ask him to put it right," explained Percy.

"Did you say *tell* Sir Topham Hatt?" asked Duck thoughtfully. There was a long silence.

"I propose," said Gordon at last, "that Percy be our —er—hum—Disputation."

"ME!" squeaked Percy. "I can't."

"Rubbish, Percy," said Henry. "It's easy."

"That's settled, then," said Gordon.

Poor Percy wished it wasn't!

* * *

When Sir Topham Hatt returned, he came to the Yard.

"Hullo, Percy! It's nice to be back."

Percy jumped. Some freight cars went flying.

"Er, y-y-yes, Sir, please, Sir."

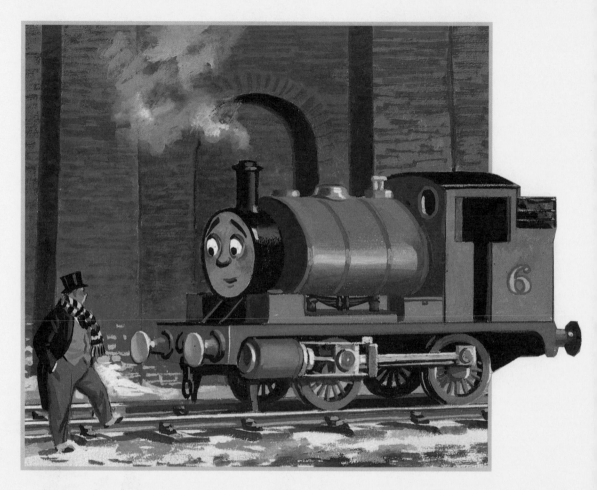

"You look nervous, Percy. What's the matter?"

"Please, Sir, they've made me a Desperation, Sir, to speak to you, Sir. I don't like it, Sir."

Sir Topham Hatt pondered. "Do you mean a Deputation, Percy?" he asked.

"Yes, Sir, please, Sir. It's Donald and Douglas, Sir.

They say, Sir, that if you send them away, Sir, they'll be turned into scrap, Sir. That'd be dreadful, Sir. Please, Sir, don't send them away, Sir. They're nice engines, Sir."

"Thank you, Percy. That will do." He walked away.

* * *

The next day, Sir Topham Hatt came to the Yard.

"I had a—er—Deputation yesterday," he said. "I understand your feelings, but I do *not* approve of interference." He paused impressively. "Donald and Douglas, I hear that your work in the snow was good. What color paint would you like?"

The twins were surprised. "Blue, Sirr, please."

"Very well. But your names will be painted on you. We'll have no more 'mistakes.'"

"Thankye, Sirr. Does this mean that the baith o' us...?"

Sir Topham Hatt smiled. "It means..."

But the rest of his speech was drowned in a delighted chorus of cheers and whistles.